THE MAJOR LEAGUE
MYSTERY

THE HEATHER REED MYSTERY SERIES

THE HEATHER REED
MYSTERY SERIES
5

THE MAJOR LEAGUE MYSTERY

REBECCA PRICE JANNEY

WORD PUBLISHING

Dallas·London·Vancouver·Melbourne

THE MAJOR LEAGUE MYSTERY

Managing Editor: Laura Minchew
Project Editor: Beverly Phillips

The characters in this book are fictional. The ballplayers
are in no way based on past or present members of
the Philadelphia Phillies baseball team.

Library of Congress Cataloging–in–Publication Data

Janney, Rebecca Price, 1957–
      The major league mystery / Rebecca Price Janney.
      p. cm. — (The Heather Reed mystery series ; #5)
      Summary: While covering the Philadelphia Phillies for a weekly
newspaper, sixteen-year-old Heather Reed investigates some suspicious
events seemingly connected to the team's new pitcher.
      ISBN 0–8499–3535–0
      [1. Mystery and detective stories. 2. Baseball—Fiction.] I. Title.
II. Series : Janney, Rebecca Price, 1957– Heather Reed mystery series ; #5.
PZ7.J2433Maj   1994
[Fic]—dc20   93–45633
                                                                                        CIP
                                                                                         AC

Printed in the United States

4 5 6 7 8 9 LBM 9 8 7 6 5 4 3 2 1

*For Larry Shenk and Richard Harpster, who
believed in a little girl with big dreams.*

*With special thanks to Tug McGraw, Leigh Tobin, and
Mike DiMuzio of the Philadelphia Phillies for their
enthusiastic assistance. Also to the Phillies ballplayers and other team personnel for their
support, and to Beverly Phillips for her
ever-present help as my editor.*

Contents

1

Swing and a Miss

Heather, you can't be serious!" Jenn McLaughlin exclaimed.

Heather Reed smiled impishly. "I sure am. I know covering a major-league baseball team sounds far-fetched," she explained, "but lots of people get an early start in their careers. When I wrote about that modeling contest for *Star Struck*,* I realized how much I like journalism." Her eyes began to shine. "Besides, I smell a mystery."

Her best friend laughed. "I should've known! Let me guess. Does it have something to do with Kevin Shirley?"

Third-baseman Kevin Shirley had been a popular Phillie since he started with the team fifteen years ago. But lately he was the center of controversy. Two weeks earlier he refused to sign autographs for a group of children with cystic fibrosis who had permission to visit the dugout before a game. The press chided him severely, and oddly, the Phillies' management seemed to encourage the criticism.

---

* Heather wrote an article for *Star Struck* magazine in *The Model Mystery*.

1

"It sure does," Heather agreed. "Kevin's been acting weird since spring training. He won't talk to the press. He refuses to sign autographs or make public appearances for charities. And he keeps mostly to himself. I want to find out what's going on."

Jenn drew her knees to her chest and wrapped her arms around them. "That isn't like him at all. He's always been so friendly. I met him once at a golf benefit I attended with Dad. Shirley was surrounded by autograph-seekers, and he signed everything they threw his way." She paused. "I admit you have a point, but how will you convince a newspaper to let you cover the Phillies?"

"If I ask *The Kirby Courier's* editor, I'll stand a much better chance than if I go to a bigger paper, like Dad's." Mr. Reed was the distinguished *Philadelphia Journal's* managing editor. Heather checked her watch. "I'd better get going. Mom asked me to make dinner tonight."

Jenn walked her to the door. "So, what's your next move?"

"I'll visit *The Courier's* editor tomorrow."

"Let me know what happens," Jenn called after her.

Heather crossed the street to her house and found her mother preparing dinner. Something smelled wonderful. "Hi, Mom! Either you're home early, or I'm late." She kissed Mrs. Reed on the cheek.

"I'm early," said the attractive pediatrician. "I discharged my patient from the hospital sooner than I expected."

A half hour later, Mr. Reed came home from work, and Heather's older brother, Brian, arrived from his summer job on a landscaping crew. Brian quickly showered, then the Reeds sat down to a spaghetti dinner. Heather waited until dessert to share her new idea.

"Dad, do you think I could get a job writing for *The Kirby Courier?*" she asked. Mr. Reed looked thoughtful. "I'm not sure, Heather. Are you considering it?"

"Uh-huh. Writing for *Star Struck* inspired me. Now I'd like to do personality features on the Phillies."

"The Phillies!" Brian stared at his sister as though she'd gone bonkers. "If you ask me, they're getting enough press over this Kevin Shirley business."

"I don't know why he doesn't sign autographs," Mrs. Reed commented. She didn't follow baseball closely, but it seemed everyone in the Philadelphia area knew and had an opinion about the Phillies' third baseman. "He used to be such a nice person."

"I know what his problem is. He got greedy," Brian retorted. "Maybe $20,000 per game made him think he's better than anybody else."

Heather didn't accept Brian's theory, but she didn't want him to know about the new mystery. He might convince their parents it wasn't a safe thing for her to do. "Mom, would it be okay with you if I got a job writing about the Phillies?"

"It does seem far-fetched," she admitted, "but I'm learning not to let anything you do surprise me," Mrs. Reed laughed.

Heather took that for a yes. "I'll talk to the editor tomorrow."

"He'll laugh you out of his office," Brian predicted.

"We'll see," she responded.

Early the next morning, Heather drove the red sedan she and Brian shared to *The Kirby Courier* office. The newspaper was located in what used to be a movie theater on Main Street. On the first floor behind large swinging doors, the presses rolled loudly as they prepared another weekly edition. Heather took a narrow, creaking staircase to the second story where cigar smoke and the smell of ink filled the air. In the sparsely furnished newsroom, two middle-aged reporters worked at aging computers.

"What do you want?" asked a blonde woman with bright pink lipstick.

"I want to see Mr. Richards," Heather said confidently.

The woman gave her a once-over. "Does he know you're coming?"

"No."

The woman surprised Heather by hollering into an enclosed room, "Some kid wants to see you, Harper!"

"Send her in," he commanded.

The woman jerked her thumb toward the editor's office, and Heather went in. His appearance surprised her. He was much shorter than she expected, and Heather couldn't begin to tell his age. Harper Richards sat in a wooden captain's chair surrounded by stacks of newspapers and computer printouts. His hair looked like the wind had arranged it. Richards' white shirt-sleeves were rolled up to the elbows and stained with ink. He nodded for her to sit in a cracked vinyl chair across from his desk. A stubby cigar burned in a grimy ashtray that said "Atlantic City."

Heather doubted the air quality index was anywhere near healthful.

"I'm Heather Reed."

"What can I do for you, Miss Reed?" he asked before he started a coughing spasm.

She decided on the direct approach. "I would like to write for *The Courier.*"

He assessed her critically. Then the editor leaned back and asked in a superior tone, "How old are you?"

Heather sat up straighter. "Sixteen."

Suddenly Harper Richards yanked open the bottom drawer of an ancient filing cabinet. Its contents bulged ominously. "Do you see these?" he demanded. Heather didn't respond. "These are the résumés of college graduates who want to work for me." He slammed the drawer shut. "What makes you think I should hire you instead?" Her prospects looked poor.

"I'll be happy to write my first stories without pay," Heather boldly offered, then handed him a notebook containing her *Star Struck* articles. The editor's expression softened as he read each story while puffing on his cigar. Then he handed them back.

"Reed, huh? Is your father Patrick Reed of *The Journal?*" Heather nodded. "I see. I'll give you two weeks to show me what you can do. If my readers like you, you're in. But understand, the pay won't be much. Now, what type of writing did you have in mind?"

"I want to do personality features on the Phillies," she blurted.

Mr. Richards raised an eyebrow. "Cheeky thing, aren't you?"

"You know how much press the Kevin Shirley incident has had. I feel people would like to know more about him and the other players, why they feel and act as they do."

The editor interrupted. "I already have a sportswriter."

"But he only covers local sports. I want to go behind the scenes with the pros. That's what people like to read about."

"Okay, okay!" he surrendered. "It might just work if you have an ounce of your father's talent. You certainly have enough hutzpah! I'll get you a press pass into the Phillies' dugout. When can you get down there?"

Heather could hardly believe her ears. "I'd like to cover their weekend series with the Cubs."

"I'll get what you need," Mr. Richards promised.

Following a few more instructions, Heather floated out of the office, already planning her first interviews. When she told her family what happened, they hugged her enthusiastically.

"So, when do you go to work?" asked Mr. Reed.

"I told Mr. Richards I could cover the Phillies' weekend series."

"Your mom and I can go to the games with you!" Mr. Reed said cheerfully.

The Reeds left the house early Friday afternoon so Heather could do her interviews. "Have a great time!" her dad said when he left them at the press entrance.

"Thanks! I'm sure I will," she responded cheerfully.

An attendant in a red and white uniform gave Heather a press pass to hang from her belt loop. Then he went over some rules and told her how to get to the dugout.

"I'm going that way myself," said a familiar voice. It belonged to *The Journal's* senior sportswriter, Dave Knox.

"Hello, Mr. Knox! I'm so glad to see you."

"A little nervous?" the dignified man asked.

"Afraid so." She smiled as they entered the elevator, and its operator whisked them down to the playing field level. "Did you see my dad?"

"I sure did."

"I bet he asked you to look out for me, right?"

"Right."

They chuckled in unison.

"Is this your first time to interview the players?" asked the elevator operator.

"Yes," Heather told her.

As the doors slid open, she said, "I hope you're not disappointed."

"Why do you think she said that?" Heather asked Mr. Knox as he led her down a concrete walkway.

He lowered his voice. "This business with Kevin Shirley has everyone on edge," he explained. "And the Ol' Man has made it worse."

"Do you mean Carl Day Springer, the owner?"

"The very one. He may be old, but his tongue and attitude are sharper than a double-edged sword. He's about to fire Kevin Shirley—and anyone who comes to his defense."

"Can he do that?" asked Heather.

"He can try. Of course, Kevin can always appeal." He gave a snort. "After all of Shirley's faithful service to the Phillies, too. You can imagine how uptight everyone is. Anyway, Heather, don't take it too personally if the players seem cranky. They have reason to be afraid of the press and the management."

Now Heather felt afraid, too. The teenager's palms grew sweaty as the huge field loomed before her. It appeared much larger to her than when she sat in the stands or watched a game on TV. Organ music blared popular hits from the upstairs levels, and the cracking of wood against hard balls made its own melody. The Chicago Cubs were taking batting practice, and the late afternoon sunlight spun its gold across the Vet—short for Veteran's Stadium.

"This way," Mr. Knox directed.

Heather went with him to the dugout, stepping gingerly around wads of gum and chewing tobacco. No players were around just then. But three coaches said brusque hellos to Dave Knox and eyed Heather curiously.

"Everything looks so different, Mr. Knox," said Heather. "I'm glad I memorized the players' and coaches' numbers; otherwise, I might not recognize them!"

"Good move," he praised her. "I thought the same thing when I first started way back in the dark ages."

Heather smiled, but not for long. Just then angry words erupted from the end of the dugout closest to the locker room. Before she could tell what was going on, a huge bat whizzed straight toward her head!

2

Dugout Dilemma

The teenager ducked just in time. For a few tense seconds, no one moved. Then players and officials appeared, and it seemed to Heather everyone was shouting.

"Are you all right?" yelled Dave Knox above the noise. He put a fatherly arm around her slim shoulders.

She nodded shakily. "I'm okay."

"Are you crazy, Mike?" A tall, bald man in his late fifties scowled at the bat-thrower.

"Button it up, Shifty," responded Phillies' manager Danny Mastrodoni.

Heather recognized them from the numbers on their uniforms. Mastrodoni was speaking to pitching coach Shifty McFeal. With the athletic-looking manager stood an ashen-faced player. He gaped in horror at the girl he'd nearly hit. He went quickly over to Heather and apologized.

"I'm so sorry!" he exclaimed. His cool, blue eyes reflected the paleness of his complexion behind round, wire-rimmed glasses. He was a tall, lean, 6 feet 4, dwarfing Heather.

The manager spoke for the player as the crowd gathered around. "Mike just got bad news." Excited voices buzzed for a few seconds, then they fell silent so he could continue. "His father was in an accident and is having surgery."

Heather realized this was tonight's starting pitcher, Mike Clausen. She supposed Danny Mastrodoni would replace him with another player.

"That's a tough break, M.C.," bull-pen coach Bill Kowalchuk remarked. "I guess you'll be going to the hospital then?"

Clausen shook his head helplessly. "They told me I couldn't do anything for him at this point and that it would be better for me to stay here."

Everyone looked surprised. Murmuring filled the dugout.

"I've advised him not to pitch," Mastrodoni told Shifty McFeal.

The big player waved him off. "Thanks, Danny, but it would be worse sitting around waiting for news." He turned toward Heather again. "Hey, I'm really sorry about that bat." He was beside himself for losing his temper. "I had no right to do that, no matter how upset I was. Are you sure you're all right?"

"I'm fine. And I accept your apology."

Heather became the center of attention when Clausen asked who she was and why she was there. Dave Knox made the introductions.

"Guys, I'd like you to meet Heather Reed. Her father is my boss at *The Journal,* and she's trying her hand with *The Kirby Courier.*"

Since it wasn't a formal social situation, the players didn't introduce themselves. They just tipped their caps and nodded in her direction. Most of them seemed pre-occupied and soon went about their business. Then Dave Knox asked Heather whom she wanted to interview first.

"I know it's ambitious," she admitted, "but I'd like to talk to Pete Talarri and Juan Carreras." Both players were on hitting streaks, and she knew other reporters would be swarming around them as soon as the Phillies entered the dugout.

"I don't know that being over-ambitious has ever been a problem for you." Heather blushed. "I thought you were going to try for Kevin Shirley," he winked.

"I wish he *would* tell us what's on his mind."

Mr. Knox sniffed. "Can't say I blame him for keeping away from the press. The guy doesn't feel like signing autographs one day, and the papers make a federal case out of it the next."

"But you wrote about it," Heather protested.

"True. Ignoring it would have been like writing about the dogcatcher's race on the day we elect a president. But I didn't tear Shirley to pieces. The guy just had a bad day."

"I think there's more to it than that." Heather grew thoughtful, then added, "He really hasn't been himself since spring training."

Dave Knox smiled. "I think you believe there's a mystery here, Heather Reed!"

"Yes, I do."

"I'll be glad to help if I can," he offered. "For now, though, let me see if I can round up Talarri and Carreras for you." He rose to get them.

While she waited for the players, Heather readied her pocket-sized tape recorder for the interviews. She also kept an eye out for Kevin Shirley. She spotted him once, but the handsome player went straight to the field for warm-up exercises, then headed back to the locker room without talking to anyone. *I wonder if I'll ever get a chance to talk to him?* she thought.

In spite of her near-miss with Mike Clausen's bat and the dispirited mood in the dugout, Heather was enjoying herself enormously. She felt excited by all the activity around her. She did pause long enough, however, to pray silently that Mike Clausen's father would have successful surgery.

Mr. Knox brought both hot-hitting ballplayers to his young friend, and Heather asked them the questions she had carefully prepared. Although Juan Carreras had some difficulty speaking English, he and Heather were patient with each other.

Catcher Pete Talarri was a blast. The big player smiled and teased his way through the interview. Heather remembered his reputation as the Phillies' practical joker and took his needling in stride.

The time went so quickly that before Heather knew it, the dugout attendant walked over and said, "Miss, you'll have to leave now." She gathered her things and hopped off the bench. Since Dave Knox wasn't around, she would have to find the press box on her own.

Heather remembered coming through a tunnel to the playing field, but now she noticed two similar passageways! With some anxiety, the teenager decided to try the one nearest the dugout. Heading in that direction, she caught Pete Talarri's eye. He nodded approvingly at her choice.

Heather hurried down the hallway, her sandals clicking against the concrete. Then she came to a closed door. *It wasn't shut the first time,* she fretted. A sign on it read, "No press allowed 30 minutes before game time." *Maybe if I hurry, no one will see me.*

Heather impulsively opened the door—and froze in shock. This wasn't the home-plate runway after all. It was the locker room! Heather wanted to flee, but she couldn't get her legs to move.

"Hey!" one player yelled. "Get that girl out of here!"

Heather let go of the door and scurried back to the dugout like a mouse with a cat on its tail. On the way to freedom and safety, she caught sight of Pete Talarri laughing so hard he clutched at his sides.

"Thanks a lot," Heather remarked.

"Initiation fee!" he shouted.

The elevator operator delivered the young sportswriter to the press box on the stadium's fourth level. She gingerly entered the open-air room. A counter ran the entire length of it on two separate levels. Huge "windows" opened to the breezy night air, and journalists sat facing them, pounding away at their lap top computers.

"You're new, eh?" asked a rotund man in his forties.

"Yes. I'm Heather Reed with *The Kirby Courier.*" She tried to sound professional, despite how shaken she still felt from the practical joke.

The players had just taken the field, and Heather had a commanding view. The radio announcers with their sophisticated headsets broadcasted the action only a few feet away.

"I'm Steve Ferris, the press box assistant. Here are all the stats and news for tonight's game."

She took the small stack of papers he extended. "Thank you." She was about to ask where she should sit when Dave Knox came over and invited her to watch the game with him.

The teenager followed him to a molded plastic chair. From there Mr. Knox introduced her to the other writers within earshot.

Heather stayed in the press box for the first five innings as Mike Clausen pitched himself in and out of jams. His concentration was clearly off. Then she excused herself and went to the stands in search of her parents. She wanted to see the rest of the game with them.

"What was all that commotion down there right after Dave Knox took you to the dugout?" her father asked.

She told them both about the bat incident, emphasizing the problem with Mike Clausen's father so they wouldn't be too upset about it.

"I'm sure that was terrible news for him," Mrs. Reed commented, "but it still didn't give him a reason to throw the bat like that."

"That's what he said when he apologized," Heather responded.

"He's pitching badly," remarked her father. "His fast ball's too slow, and he keeps missing the strike zone."

Heather agreed. "I bet Danny Mastrodoni won't leave him in much longer."

He didn't. When the tormented Clausen loaded the bases with only one out, the fans got restless.

"Pull the bum!" a guy near Heather yelled.

As if in response, Danny Mastrodoni called a time out and walked slowly toward the pitcher's mound. Mike Clausen handed the ball to his manager, who slapped him on the back.

"Now pitching for the Phillies is number 46, Joe Dimitrio," said Lance Sawyer, the stadium announcer.

"He's new," Heather told her parents. "He just came up from the minor-league team in Reading."

Dimitrio struck out both batters, which ended Chicago's threat. A wild cheer went up for him after he secured a 5–4 victory in the next four innings.

"What a guy!" Mr. Reed exclaimed as they flowed with the crowd out of the stadium.

"I'll say!" Heather chimed in. "Normally a manager won't let a new reliever pitch that long, but he was so good."

"I think you should interview him," her dad encouraged.

"I think you're right," Heather agreed.

The next morning she eagerly searched the paper and listened to the radio for information about Mike Clausen's father but learned nothing. After breakfast, she worked on her first article for *The Courier.* Since it was Saturday, her father was at home and offered to proofread it.

"Except for those two typos and the vague quote in the third paragraph, it's terrific," he praised. "I think you do quite well."

"Thanks, Dad," Heather smiled. "Are you and Mom going with me this afternoon, too?"

"I will," he said. "Your mother wants to do some shopping. By the way, we decided if this job becomes permanent, you'll need to take someone with you to the stadium. We don't want you driving down there alone."

Heather started to protest, but she closed her mouth when she saw how determined her dad looked. "I understand," she conceded.

In the dugout late that afternoon Heather tried in vain to get Joe Dimitrio away from other reporters so she could talk to him. *It hardly seems fair,* she brooded. *They have access to him in the locker room after the game, but this is the only time I have with the players.*

Then Heather saw Mike Clausen emerge from the tunnel near the locker room and walk into the dugout. Seeing Heather, he smiled shyly and walked toward her.

"I see I didn't scare you away," he joked.

"Nah. How's your dad, Mike?"

He sat down next to her. "You didn't hear it on the radio?"

Heather hadn't heard the news since leaving the house. She shook her head.

"The strangest thing happened. Last night after I left the game, I showered and was about to leave for the hospital when the P.R. guy called me to the phone. It was a nurse. She was listening to the game and heard about my dad being at her hospital. She was really surprised—my dad wasn't there!"

3

Inside Track

Heather's mouth fell open. "Your dad *wasn't* there?"

"No."

"What happened?" Although this sounded like a scoop, she didn't turn on her tape recorder. Because she respected his privacy, Mike responded more openly to her.

"The first thing I did was call my parents' house. It turned out my dad was there. He was fine except for hearing on the radio about an accident he'd never had! The attending physician in the hospital said there must've been a mix-up."

"But why didn't your dad call you when he heard about it on the radio?" Heather asked.

Clausen shrugged. "He left a message, but it never got to me. Sometimes that happens during a game, but I was pretty upset over the whole thing."

"With whom did he leave the message?"

"I guess someone in public relations." His expression suddenly hardened as two other reporters came over and started asking questions. "That's all there is to it," he

insisted. "You guys are making too big a deal over this."
The tall pitcher got up from the bench and hurried onto
the field where his teammates took batting practice.

I don't blame him, Heather thought. *He probably
doesn't want to be the next Kevin Shirley. I guess what
happened could've been a practical joke, but I don't think
it was at all funny. Wouldn't that person have come forward by now? And why didn't the P.R. people get him that
message? The whole thing doesn't sound right to me. I
think there's something weird going on with the Phillies.*

"Hey, kid!" A journalist addressed the teenager. "What
did M.C. tell you?"

Heather felt reluctant to share the information. "Just
that it was a mix-up," she told them.

"Who are you anyway?" another one asked.

Heather introduced herself and fell into a lively conversation with the other reporters. Before she had a chance
to talk to the new reliever, Joe Dimitrio, it was time for
Heather to go to the press box. This time she found her
way there without difficulty. But since Dave Knox was
off that afternoon, Heather wasn't sure where to sit. She
waited for Steve Ferris, the press box attendant, to tell her
where she could sit. "On the first level," he instructed.
"There are lots of places over there on the right."

"Oh, by the way," Heather asked before Ferris could
get away, "I'd like to have one of those media guides."
She had seen Dave Knox's copy the night before and
wanted one. The guide was a spiral-bound team direc-
tory full of Phillies' information.

"Sure," he responded. "I'll see that you get one."

Heather thanked him and took her place. During the top of the third inning, someone came over and introduced himself.

"Excuse me." Standing before her was a man in his early twenties. He wore his short brown hair in a shaggy way and sported a pair of horn-rimmed glasses that seemed much too old for his wide, young face. His narrow eyes were hazel like Heather's, and he wore a suit. Not many sportswriters dressed that formally.

"Are you Heather Reed?" he asked.

"Yes." She was surprised he knew.

"Steve Ferris asked me to give this to you." He handed her the media guide.

"Oh, thank you!" she gushed. "This is wonderful."

"I'm John Krauss, the Public Relations assistant."

Heather offered her hand for him to shake. "Nice to meet you." She was immediately interested because of the episode with Mike Clausen's father. "That was some mix-up last night, wasn't it?" she asked.

"Oh, that. It was unfortunate," he remarked. Krauss leaned against the chair next to Heather's and asked how she liked her new job.

"It's terrific," she said.

"Glad to hear it. How are the players toward you?"

"I'm not sure what you mean."

"Are they giving you the time of day?"

"Yes. Are they that nervous about the press?"

"Wouldn't you be?"

The reporters sitting nearby shot him dirty looks, but he didn't appear to notice.

"Well, they've been nice to me," Heather informed him. She noticed Kevin Shirley had just struck out and recorded a "K" on her score card of the game. "I just wish I could get near Joe Dimitrio."

Krauss seemed interested. "What's the problem?"

"There's no problem, really. I want to interview him because he's doing so well, but everyone else has the same idea. And because I can't get into the clubhouse, I don't have as much access to him as other reporters."

"I'll take care of that."

"Actually, I don't want to go into the clubhouse," she corrected. "I just need time with Joe Dimitrio before a game."

"Certainly. Will you be here tomorrow?"

"Yes."

"I'll arrange for you to see Joe then."

"You will?"

"Hey, that's what I get paid for," he laughed. "Can you get here early?"

"Not too early. I go to church on Sundays."

The young man pursed his lips. "Well, come as soon as you can then."

"Thank you," Heather said. Although she considered John Krauss's manner a bit stiff, she appreciated his help. He astonished her when he sat down and asked her some personal questions. Heather really just wanted to watch the game and felt awkward with his boldness. Krauss finally left during the seventh inning stretch.

On Sunday Heather went to church in the morning and hurried with her parents to the game immediately afterward. But she still got there too late to see Joe Dimitrio. John Krauss assured Heather she could see him the next time she came, if she got there early enough.

The Phillies wrapped up the series with the Cubs, winning two games and losing another. Dimitrio pitched the wins, and the whole city buzzed about his talent.

Heather turned in her first story about Pete Talarri and Juan Carreras Monday afternoon, and they ran in Wednesday's *Kirby Courier.* That day she drove to a convenience store and bought five copies. Quickly turning to the sports section, she thrilled at the sight of her name on the page and marveled that Mr. Richards barely edited the piece. *I have Dad to thank for that,* she smiled to herself.

That night her parents took Heather to dinner at her favorite restaurant in King of Prussia to celebrate. "But I don't have the job yet," she protested.

"This is good enough for us," Mr. Reed insisted. "We're very proud of your accomplishment."

Two days later Harper Richards called Heather. "You did a good job," he said gruffly. "You write well, and so far the response looks favorable."

"Then I'm in?" she asked.

"I said two weeks, and I meant it," the editor said firmly. "I want to see how you can handle a tough assignment." Heather gulped. "Get me an interview with Carl Day Springer. Then I'll decide."

The teenager lifted her chin and spoke confidently. "I'll do it," she promised.

But getting to see the Phillies' controversial owner wasn't easy. Heather had to wait all day for Springer's secretary to return her phone call. At 5:30, it finally came. Carl Day Springer would see Heather the following Tuesday at 4:00 P.M.

On Saturday, Heather got her opportunity to interview Joe Dimitrio. Unfortunately, he only had five minutes to spare.

"I know you want more time to talk," he said, "but I can't make this long today. When will you be back?"

Heather planned to attend the Tuesday game after her meeting with Carl Day Springer. "Three days from now," she told the relief pitcher. She felt slightly frustrated.

"I'll see you then. Can you get here before batting practice?"

"I'll try," she said.

"That would be best for me. Sorry about the delay!"

Because Dimitrio acted so friendly about the whole thing, Heather didn't mind waiting as much. In the meantime, she decided to get some information about him through the pitching coach. *He should have something interesting to say about Joe. After all, Shifty works with Joe more than anyone else on the team,* she reasoned.

The next time Shifty McFeal—so-named because of his beady-looking eyes and craftiness as a baseball player thirty years before—came by, Heather stopped him.

"I'd like to ask you some questions about Joe Dimitrio," she explained.

Shifty sat next to her, showing his answer was yes. The pitching coach didn't talk much.

"You must be very pleased with him," she offered.

"Yup."

"What do you think is his greatest strength?"

"His fast ball," said the coach.

Oh, boy! Heather thought. *This is going to be tough.* "I've been wondering, since he's doing so well, will you move him from relief work to the starting rotation?"

Shifty thought about that for a moment then answered, "Can't say for sure. He's good, but he tires easily."

Finally! More than three syllables! Heather smiled to herself. "Isn't that odd for someone his age?"

The coach shrugged. "Maybe. Some guys aren't meant to be starters."

They talked for a few more minutes; that is, Heather talked for a few more minutes. Then Shifty joined the players on the field. *At least I have some good material to work with,* Heather thought. *Maybe Joe will tell me more on Tuesday. I'll wait until then to write the story.*

Monday morning Heather poured over newspapers and baseball magazines looking for information on Carl Day Springer. She found an abundance of articles about him. Most of the writers didn't seem to like him much, though they were careful about how they said so. *Out of fear?* Heather wondered. *If so, what do they have to be afraid of? Of course, Mr. Springer is powerful in Philadelphia. Maybe he could get them fired.*

Jenn McLaughlin finally pulled her best friend away from her homework on the Phillies. But even when the two teenagers hung out at the swim club, their friends came over and started arguing about the team. Heather's new friend Evan Templeton was there, too. She discovered that he had once lived in Kevin Shirley's neighborhood.

"I used to deliver his paper," Evan said.

"What was he like?" asked Heather.

"I always thought he was friendly. I think it's a shame he got so selfish."

"Maybe he was just tired," another friend suggested. "I'll bet those guys don't always want to sign autographs."

"They should for that kind of money," charged still another.

Jenn looked at Heather and rolled her eyes. "I can't get you away from the Phillies, can I?"

On her way to Veteran's Stadium Tuesday afternoon, Heather stopped by her dad's office at *The Philadelphia Journal* to see if Dave Knox was available. He had been around baseball all his life. She hoped he could advise her on how to interview Carl Day Springer.

"For the competition, eh?" he teased.

"Hardly." Heather gave a laugh. "Comparing *The Courier* to *The Journal* is like comparing the Phillies to Kirby High's baseball team!"

"Very well." The veteran sportswriter leaned against a window. "Springer's a tough guy. He's always stirred up controversy. He pushes people around and expects them to jump at his command. Not everyone appreciates that style of leadership."

Heather interrupted. "How did he get to be the Phillies' owner?"

"Inherited the position."

"And he's reigned supreme ever since?"

"That is correct."

Heather paused. "Mr. Knox, how do you think I should approach him?"

The sportswriter snorted. "I suggest you say your prayers before going up there."

"So I should be on my guard?" Heather asked.

"I strongly suggest it."

"Another thing. I'd like to talk to him about Kevin Shirley. Do you think that would be wise?"

Her mentor frowned. "You'll need to be the judge of that. It could go either way."

She thanked Mr. Knox for his time and briefly visited with her father. He wished her well. "I'll take the train to Veteran's Stadium after work," he concluded. "When the game ends, we can meet at the press gate. That way we can go home together."

"Thanks, Dad," Heather commented. "But I really do okay by myself."

Her father became firm. "Honey, if you're to do this very grown-up job, you'll need to do it according to your mother's and my guidelines." He tilted his head and looked at her pleasantly, but uncompromisingly.

"Okay." Heather kissed her dad on the cheek and left.

On the way to the ball park, the teenager tuned in to the local sports station and heard a startling announcement. "This bulletin just in from Veteran's Stadium," said the broadcaster. "Phillies' owner Carl Day Springer has fired Kevin Shirley. I repeat . . ."

"So he did it after all!" Heather said aloud. She listened for details.

"However, Shirley has filed an appeal through the Players' Association, and he can play pending a decision."

Heather felt sympathy for Shirley. *He's always been my favorite Phillie, and I'm sure he wouldn't act like he does without good reason.*

"Give the guy a break!" one caller to the talk show exclaimed. "This isn't the end of the world, you know."

"Those kids thought so," a woman caller retorted. "He's selfish and petty."

After several minutes, Heather tired of the broadcast and tuned in a news station. But it reported on the Kevin Shirley story, too! *I think Mr. Springer could be creating this uproar,* she considered. *Maybe it's his way of unloading an expensive player. I've read that he hates how much money today's players make. Hopefully I can find out. Maybe there's some way I can help Kevin Shirley . . . if he's innocent.*

Heather reached Veterans Stadium fifteen minutes early and parked near the press gate. She obtained her pass and went to the owner's office on the fourth floor. She just stepped off the elevator and was about to address the receptionist in the busy lobby when she heard nasty yelling down the hall. Heather listened intently. "I've tried to reason with you, but you won't listen!" cried one man.

"You call that reason?" bellowed the other.

"He's like a sheep for the slaughter, and you're encouraging it, Mr. Springer."

"Don't you point at me! I'll bury you!"

4

Not-So-Empty Threats

A well-dressed man in his thirties charged down the hall with the speed of a Joe Dimitrio fast ball.

I wonder who that was? Heather asked herself. She took a deep breath and approached the startled-looking receptionist who quickly put on a smile for her.

"How may I help you?"

"I'm Heather Reed from *The Kirby Courier.* I have an appointment with Mr. Springer."

The pretty woman's expression said, *Good luck!* But she said, "Please have a seat."

Heather went to a leather couch and waited. A glass-encased cabinet boasted Phillies' memorabilia. Photos of the Springer family with famous Phillies and political dignitaries, including six U.S. presidents, decked the walls. Heather shivered. Carl Day Springer was, after all, an ominous personality.

Just then a middle-aged woman in a navy suit beckoned Heather. "Mr. Springer will see you now," she announced.

The teenager followed her down a narrow hallway flanked by offices. They stopped at a door with a plaque bearing Springer's name and title in brass. Heather entered a large office glowing with rich mahogany furniture and highly polished brass fixtures. Her feet sank into the forest-green carpet. Just beyond his office, a short hallway led into Springer's exclusive box from which he viewed the ball games.

Carl Day impatiently motioned her to sit across from him, giving her the impression he wanted to be done with this tiresome duty. He sat in a green, leather chair behind a massive, antique desk. The elderly man made no move to shake her hand. That failure of courtesy imparted fresh courage to Heather. She sat up a little straighter as she turned on the tape recorder.

"What do you want?" he asked bluntly.

"You agreed to an interview with *The Kirby Courier*," she reminded him.

"So I did." He looked up, and his keen blue eyes bored into her gaze. Heather refused to blink.

"I'm new with the press, so I appreciate that you made time for me," she said politely.

"I meet every reporter who comes to this team," he stated with obvious pride. "And if you do things my way, we'll get along just fine."

That sounds suspicious, Heather thought. "Could we start with Kevin Shirley, sir?"

His eyes blazed. "Shirley is finished in this town!"

"Are you mostly upset with his behavior?" Heather asked.

"Yes!" he exploded. "He has no right to act like such a prima donna. I made him. I gave him a chance on this team when the coaches said he didn't have a future. Now he refuses to sign autographs for sick kids!"

"Do you think the Players' Association will back him up?"

"Of course they will. They're thicker than thieves with these baseball players and their fat agents." His right index finger jabbed at the air. "But I don't have to play that game."

The threatening words startled Heather. "Is that on the record, Mr. Springer?"

"Yes! I want everyone to know where I stand. These ballplayers have no right to cause trouble," he bellowed. "They get paid well enough. I expect them to come and do their jobs without fanfare. That guy who was just in here?" Heather listened in excitement. "That was Shirley's bubble-headed agent. He disagrees with my methods. But I do what I like. These players nowadays don't respect authority." His tone softened slightly. "If Shirley would apologize and act right, I'd bring him back. I'm a fair man, don't you think?"

"You think so," Heather said as respectfully as she could.

He didn't like it. Springer wanted no less than her agreement. "And I think it's time for you to go," he stated bluntly. He made no move to rise and see Heather to the door.

She got up and extended her hand. The Phillies' owner took it reluctantly. "Thank you for your time," she said stiffly.

On her way to the dugout, Heather replayed the con-versation in her mind. She concluded that Springer had harsh and negative feelings toward baseball players in general. He didn't like their attitudes and deeply resented their salaries. He also expected them to do anything he asked. *He really does believe he owns them—in every sense of the word,* she thought.

In addition, Springer also wasn't above making threats to keep them under his thumb. *Might harassment, such as telling a starting pitcher his father's being rushed into surgery, be one way to keep the players on edge?* She wondered.

Heather walked past the receptionist, then out to the elevator and pushed the down button. While waiting, she thought about the hateful meeting between Kevin Shirley's agent and Mr. Springer. *I doubt Carl Day Springer respects professional baseball's rules for player appeals. He may try to make life so miserable for Kevin Shirley that Kevin won't even want to stay. Oh, I'd love to talk to Kevin and get his side of the story!* Heather sighed. The chances of that happening appeared dismal since most of the press had skunked him.

Because everything the owner had told her was "on the record," Heather thought she had the makings of an exciting story. She hoped Mr. Richards would be pleased enough with it to hire her permanently.

"Hello, Heather," Clara, the elevator operator, smiled at the teenager.

"Oh, hi!" She was surprised the woman knew her name.

"How are you?"

"Just fine," Heather responded.

"I hope you have your umbrella," she warned. "It looks like rain."

When Heather got to the field, dark clouds roamed the sky above Veteran's Stadium. Just as she sat in the dugout, a downpour started. The ground crew sprang into action and within minutes had the infield covered in shiny red tarp. Because batting practice couldn't proceed outdoors, most of the players retreated to the clubhouse or the indoor batting cage. Only a few were willing to chat with the reporters who hovered around the dugout for interviews. Heather guessed they were still afraid of saying the wrong thing about Kevin Shirley to the press.

Her thoughts were interrupted when second baseman Pete Manning walked up to Heather and stared at her. She felt uneasy when he made no move to leave. Was he trying to threaten her? She wasn't sure, but every time she moved away, Manning followed.

"Just what do you think you're doing?" she demanded.

"Are you a girl?" he asked rudely.

Heather got sarcastic with Manning. "What do you think?"

"I believe I'll take you with me," he said evenly.

The handsome Phillie took his sweaty cap off and shoved it over Heather's carefully styled hair. She turned her nose up at the odor and tried to whip it off, but Pete Manning pushed it down again, this time covering her eyes. Then he effortlessly picked up the teenager with one arm and held the cap in place with his other hand.

Heather began pounding on the big ballplayer. That didn't stop him.

Then she heard someone say sternly, "Cut it out, Manning!"

Heather thought she recognized manager Danny Mastrodoni's voice.

"Oh, c'mon, Danny! I'm just having a little fun," defended the offender.

"You heard me!"

"Oh, all right," the player whined.

He set Heather down feet-first on the dugout floor and removed his cap from her head. Without apologizing, he strolled off to the locker room. Heather smoothed her rumpled outfit and resumed her place on the bench, red-faced.

"Are you all right?" Joe Dimitrio asked with concern.

"Yes," she said tightly.

"He shouldn't do stuff like that." He shook his head and left.

Then Heather realized she had missed a golden opportunity to talk with him. *I was so angry I wasn't thinking clearly,* she fretted.

A few minutes later, the young public relations assistant came over and sat next to her. "Don't let him get to you," John Krauss said. "Manning likes to intimidate the ladies."

"Nice guy," Heather muttered.

"I think he's a moron," Krauss spat. "Half these guys are, you know. I'd say you handled him pretty well. Not all the women who come in here do."

"You mean he does that to every . . ." her voice trailed off in disbelief.

He nodded solemnly. "He doesn't like having them in the dugout. You should see how mean he gets with the ones who go into the clubhouse. Especially now. They're all running scared after Shirley got canned. Except Dimitrio. He's a minimally paid rookie who gives a thousand percent. Say," he wondered, "did you ever get to talk to him?"

"Oh, John, I just missed the chance!"

"Wait right here," he smiled.

Moments later Krauss appeared with the twenty-four-year-old rookie. Other reporters flocked to him like rabbits to a carrot patch. Dimitrio flashed his winning smile, revealing straight, white teeth. She also saw a scar by his right ear. Heather had never been close enough to him to notice it before.

Dimitrio waved off the other newspeople with a laugh. "I promised this young lady an interview."

Heather enjoyed talking to the charming player about his recent success. They discussed the batters who challenged him most and his favorite pitches. However, he looked at his watch when the teenager asked about his background.

"I'm sorry, Heather, but I've gotta get back to the clubhouse."

"Could we finish another time?" she inquired.

He hesitated. "Maybe. See ya later!"

After he left, John Krauss came back, "Isn't he terrific? That guy is going to save this team. I just wish the rest of these clowns were like him."

"John, is there any chance I can talk to Kevin Shirley?"

Krauss laughed cynically. "About as much chance as interviewing the President of the United States." Then his manner became confidential. "And I hear he isn't mixing too well with his teammates either. He ought to pack his bags. If it weren't for him, the team would be more focused on baseball and playing better than .500," meaning the Phillies would be winning more than half their games.

Heather regarded him in wonder. *Why is he telling me this stuff? He hardly knows me! He has no guarantee I won't blab it all over the paper. Maybe he wants me to. Maybe he's in league with Carl Day Springer.*

"You're a good journalist," John Krauss smiled. "You have potential to make it big."

Heather was surprised—again. "Thanks. Do you live close enough to get *The Courier?*"

"Let's just say you're worth my time." Again, the winning smile.

Why? she asked herself. *Something isn't right about this.*

Heather was about to probe deeper when Dave Knox came over. She wished Krauss would leave so she could tell Mr. Knox about her interview with the Phillies' owner. She also wanted to ask her older friend what he thought of the P.R. assistant. Ten minutes later, Krauss excused himself. Just as Heather opened her mouth, however, frantic activity arrested everyone's attention.

Pitcher Jose Mansano fled from the clubhouse, past the dugout, and down the first base line. Close behind was another pitcher, Bib Shoon, his face red with anger, wielding a hefty bat! Heather and everyone else in the dugout gawked. In full view of the entire stadium Shoon pursued his teammate, who barely stayed ahead of the menacing bat and its owner.

"Are they serious?" Heather asked.

"I'd say so," answered Dave Knox. "I've never seen Bib like that before."

I wonder what happened in the clubhouse? It's so tense around here! Heather thought.

The young reporter watched breathlessly as the two players neared the dugout. Shoon grabbed Mansano's practice jersey from behind and yanked him to the ground. The force of Jose's fall sent him rolling down the four steps into the dugout. He stopped right below Heather's feet! She watched in horror as the 6-feet-3-inch Mansano lay prone on the grubby floor while Bib Shoon scurried down the steps clutching the big bat. The black-haired pitcher leered victoriously at Mansano as he stood above him.

"Mercy!" pleaded Mansano breathlessly. "Have mercy!"

Bib Shoon sneered. Muttering, "No mercy," he placed a cleated foot on Mansano's chest and prepared to jump on it with his full weight!

5

Players on the Run

Just as he moved to pounce on Jose like a stampeding elephant, Bib started laughing. Then Jose easily pushed him off. He sprang up, and the men engaged in a playful wrestling match. Heather sighed with relief as the pitchers howled and scuffled like school boys at recess, unaware of the anxiety they had caused the reporters.

"I'm getting too old for this." Dave Knox mopped his forehead with a crisp, white handkerchief.

"Mr. Knox, would everyone have reacted so tensely before the controversy this season?" Heather asked.

He became thoughtful. "I doubt it. Ballplayers always egg each other on. They seem to get along best when they're teasing and roughhousing." He sighed. "I haven't seen one shaving-cream-pie-in-the-face stunt all year."

"Do you think Kevin Shirley is the source of the trouble?"

"That's a good question. I'm really not sure."

Heather quickly told Dave Knox about her interview with Mr. Springer. "Do you think he could be behind all the problems?" she asked.

"I suppose that's possible," Knox said. "He does act outlandish at times. But for all his bluster, I've never known him to generate pure meanness. You know, Heather, the more I think about it, the more I trace the team's tension back to Kevin Shirley."

"Do you think Kevin's in the wrong?"

"I've known him a long time," the sportswriter considered. "He's always been such a gentleman. If he is in the wrong, as you say, I doubt it's entirely his fault. Springer can be a stubborn mule." Knox slapped his hands against his knees. "I need some food. How about joining me for dinner?"

"I'd love to!"

They went up to the busy dining room behind the press box and enjoyed a leisurely meal. An hour later the weather cleared up, and the crew chief—the home-plate umpire—yelled, "Play ball!"

By the top of the second inning, the San Diego Padres led 4–3. In the fourth, the harassed Kevin Shirley bobbled a ball at third, and the Padre hitter made it to first safely on his error. The fans booed Shirley loudly. Heather thought it was to the third baseman's credit that he didn't let it ruin his concentration. When the next hitter sent a bullet back to him, Shirley initiated a brilliant double play that got the Phillies out of scoring trouble. Half the fans cheered while the other half booed.

The Padres' pitcher had been throwing wild all evening. But he made one close shave too many in the sixth inning. Matt Parker sent a fast ball right into Pete Manning's shoulder. The big second baseman went down hard and writhed in pain. Center fielder Phil Hollister charged the pitcher from the on-deck circle and shoved him so hard the man stumbled off the pitcher's mound. The Padre catcher ran to Parker's assistance and took a swing at Hollister.

The rest of the scene was a blur of arms and fists as Heather watched what became a bench-clearing brawl between the two teams. It was twenty minutes before all four umpires, the managers and coaches restored order. The crew chief ejected both Phil Hollister and the Padres' catcher from the game.

The Phillies' defense totally disintegrated. Kenny Scribner's pitching became so irregular that Danny Mastrodoni yanked him in the bottom of the eighth inning with just one out and Padres on first and second bases. Then he brought in the rookie sensation, Joe Dimitrio.

The first batter grounded out. The second one hit a long fly into right field, and Larry Carlsen handled it easily. When the Phillies got up to bat, Juan Carreras hit a single. Then shortstop Lefty Washington nailed a double. More surprising was the double Joe Dimitrio smashed when Danny Mastrodoni allowed Dimitrio to bat for himself. That scored two runs, and the Phillies forged ahead, 5–4.

They ran into trouble again in the ninth when Willie Boaz committed an error, and the Padres had the tying run on first base. The player stole second. The Padres' home-run hitter, Juice Emory, hammered the ball into center field. Alex Sciascia, substituting for Phil Hollister, caught it at the warning track. Then he hurled the ball with all his might back toward the infield where the Padre runner charged toward home plate. Lefty Washington caught the relay and speared it to catcher Pete Talarri. In the closest of plays, the home plate umpire loudly declared the base runner out. The Phillies won the game!

Heather watched the instant replay on the press box monitor and saw that the umpire had made a good call on the close play. *Especially if you're a Phillies fan!* she smiled to herself.

The regular press headed quickly for the clubhouse where they hoped to interview the star of the game, Joe Dimitrio. Heather cleaned up her things and hurried to the press gate to meet her father.

The next evening as Heather's family began cleaning up the dinner dishes, the phone rang. Brian answered it.

"Yes, she is. Who's calling please?" he asked. He put his hand over the receiver. "Heather, it's a guy named John Krauss."

She put the last drinking glass into the dishwasher and took the phone from her brother. "Hi, John. Uh-huh. Yes, I'll probably be around. You did what?" Heather couldn't believe her ears. John had told her editor at *The Courier* that she was an asset to the Phillies. And Richards had told John that he planned to keep Heather on board. The teenager couldn't help wondering why John Krauss would have such an interest in her.

"Stick with me, and you'll do just fine," he boasted.

Heather quickly lost interest in the conversation and twirled a piece of hair around her finger impatiently as he droned on and on without pausing for air. She kept waiting for an opening to tell him she wanted to go. Then Krauss said something that aroused her interest.

"It's tough doing P.R. with this team's problems. They won't last much longer, though. I'm going to put a stop to it if it's the last thing I do!" he vowed.

6

Unwelcome Attention

O h, really?" Heather eagerly awaited John Krauss's explanation.

"What?" Brian asked, leaning closer.

Heather waved him off.

"The players' wives are going to put on a Phillies Fun Fair. The proceeds will go to Children's Medical Center," he said smugly. "It's time this team got some positive press."

"I think you have a good idea," Heather said. She felt disappointed the news wasn't more stimulating.

"There's more," he continued. "In a few weeks we'll host a media softball contest between games of a double-header. The print media will play the broadcast reporters. Will you be on the print media's team?"

"I'd love to," she told Krauss.

He gave her a few details about the match. Then Heather excused herself and hung up. Turning around, she laughed; her mother, father, and brother stared at her inquisitively.

"I'm not the only one around here with a major case of curiosity!" She laughed.

"Well, what happened?" Brian goaded. "Since we're being nosy, we might as well do it thoroughly."

"John Krauss did the oddest thing," his sister replied. "He called Mr. Richards at *The Courier* and told him I'm an asset to the ball club. He talked my editor into keeping me on, although Mr. Richards told John he planned to keep me anyway." She laughed and shook her head. "I'm really surprised."

Her brother sniffed disapprovingly. "I think he likes you."

"Heather, is there something you want to tell us?" asked her concerned father.

"No, Dad. I haven't the slightest interest in him. John's too old for me. He's at least twenty-three."

"Well, I'm relieved to hear that," Mrs. Reed sighed. "I knew you had more sense than to develop an interest in an older man."

Heather hugged her parents. "Thanks for believing in me. I'm going over to Jenn's for a while."

She hurried across the street where her friend's little brothers Timmy and Geoff pounced on Heather at the front door with questions about the Phillies.

"Heather, did you really meet Mike Clausen?" asked eight-year-old Timmy breathlessly.

"I told you she did," complained Geoff, four years older. "Do you think you could get us some autographs?" He was an avid baseball card collector and, even at his age, knew more trivia about players than many older enthusiasts.

Heather smiled. "I'll see what I can do. Which players' autographs do you want?"

"Joe Dimitrio," both said.

"Well! I'm surprised. Why not one of the stars—like Mike Clausen or Juan Carreras?" She didn't even suggest Kevin Shirley.

"'Cause he's gonna be big time!" exclaimed Timmy enthusiastically. "He's great!"

Heather said she would try, and the boys hurried to the coat closet to get baseballs for Dimitrio to sign. They returned with a dozen.

"Whoa, there! Let's start with one apiece." Heather took two balls. "Where's Jenn? Oh, hi, Mrs. McLaughlin."

Jenn's mother entered the spacious foyer on her way to the living room. "Heather, are these boys pestering you for autographs? That's all I've been hearing lately."

Heather smiled. "I don't mind. Where's Jenn?"

"Outside on the deck," she pointed.

Heather excused herself and went out back to find her best friend, who was reading a fashion magazine. "What's happening with the Phillies?" Jenn asked.

Heather brought her up to date. "I have an uneasy feeling someone wants to keep tripping up the team," she concluded.

"It's possible," her friend agreed. "So, who's your chief suspect and why?"

"Right now it's Carl Day Springer. He's so hard on Kevin Shirley, and I don't think he's above getting rid of him dishonestly. He told Shirley's agent, 'I'll bury you.'"

"Well, Kevin is stuck-up," Jenn said in disgust.

"I'm not so sure." Heather thought deeply for a moment. "Of course, he does have a motive for disrupting the team."

"You mean like that fake call about Mike Clausen's dad?"

"Uh-huh. Maybe he wants to get back at Mr. Springer for publicly coming down hard on him," Heather explained. She paused then added, "I'm also suspicious of John Krauss. He said it was just a misunderstanding when I asked about the Mike Clausen thing. He hurried off before I could ask more questions. And why would he be interested in a sixteen-year-old girl?"

"Have you looked in the mirror lately?" asked her friend softly.

The teenagers visited for an hour, discussing other subjects, like Jenn's ongoing crush on Brian, vacation plans, and the youth group. But Heather's mind was never far from the Phillies' mystery.

When she returned to her room, Heather prepared her newspaper article on Carl Day Springer. It went quickly because he'd said so many colorful things. Then she decided to look for information on Joe Dimitrio to fill out what he had told her at the stadium. She was eager to finish a piece on him, but she needed more information.

First Heather searched the media guide and the score book Brian bought her at the stadium but found only small write-ups about Dimitrio. They mentioned how he came to the Phillies from the minor league Reading team. He had played there just one season and pitched so well the Phillies called him up. They also listed his marital status as single. Dimitrio was 6 feet 4 inches tall, weighed 220 pounds, and was twenty-four years old. He came from Columbia, Ohio, and graduated from Columbia

Area High School and Barry Community College. He lived in New Jersey.

Heather wished she had more of Dimitrio's quotes to use. Even Shifty McFeal hadn't given her much to add about the rookie. But she put together a short piece giving her impressions of the sensational young player. *It's better than nothing—or waiting for another opportunity to talk to him,* she decided.

The next day she called her editor at *The Courier.* "I hear I have a job," she said.

"How do you know?" Harper Richards asked, surprised.

"A little birdie named John Krauss told me."

A grumble came over the line. "He's impressed with you, young lady," admitted the editor. "Frankly, so am I."

"But you haven't seen the Carl Day Springer story yet," Heather mentioned.

"Doesn't matter, Miss Reed. I know you'll do a good job. Just get it to me by tomorrow. Oh, and one more thing."

"What's that?"

"I can't pay you much. Only thirty-five dollars a story."

"It's worth the experience," the teenager responded.

That afternoon Heather received a call from Rick Gerrity, the sportscaster for WPHP-TV. He wanted to interview her. Heather thanked him but declined his offer. She disliked publicity. Then Dave Knox also phoned and asked if he could do a story about her. "It isn't every day a teenage girl covers professional baseball," he coaxed.

Because Knox worked for her father's paper, Heather accepted.

Three days later, she groaned when the article appeared in *The Journal.* It mentioned that earlier in the year she had used both her writing ability and her investigating skills to solve a mystery involving participants in The American Model of the Year Contest.

"I wish I hadn't let him interview me," Heather complained to Jenn on the phone. "Last night some players avoided me."

"Because of the article?"

"I'm not sure. There was a team meeting before the game, and that cut into my time in the dugout," she admitted. "But I hate that the Phillies know I like to solve mysteries. That could ruin everything."

Then Jenn asked impishly, "Tell me, how's John Krauss?"

Heather moaned. "I'm afraid he's turning into a pest, Jenn. I really don't like him very much."

"From what you've told me, I don't think I'd like him too much either." She paused. "Did you tell Dave Knox you didn't like the story?"

"Not exactly," Heather said. "I just told him I dislike publicity because I think it will hinder my chances of getting interviews with the players. He told me not to worry."

A few minutes after Heather said good-bye to Jenn, the phone rang.

"Heather, Dave Knox here."

"Hi," she said. "What's up?"

"I just got word that Carl Day Springer has to take Kevin Shirley back," he announced.

"Do you think Kevin will stay after all the unpleasantness?"

"His agent says he will. The saga continues."

"It certainly does!" Heather thanked him for calling. *I'll bet Carl Day isn't at all pleased,* she considered. *He may just try something underhanded to get rid of Kevin Shirley now. Mr. Knox is right—the saga does continue.*

The following night Heather interviewed center fielder Phil Hollister while the veteran reporters swarmed around Joe Dimitrio. Dimitrio was pitching incredibly in relief, saving the slumping Phillies from sliding in the standings. *I'll never get to finish that interview,* Heather thought glumly. She understood why Dimitrio would rather talk to the more established reporters than to her, though.

Heather's time with Hollister ended abruptly when someone on the field yelped in pain. She focused on a group huddling around a player. The dugout emptied of other Phillies and coaches as they scurried to see who got hurt.

I'm dying to find out what happened, Heather thought. *But I don't want to get in the way.* She decided to stay put, straining to see beyond the wall of red and white uniforms.

Ten minutes later Hollister came back. "I think we're jinxed," he moaned, shaking his head back and forth.

"What happened?" Heather asked eagerly.

"Felix's pitching hand got hit."

Felix Undeljar, an excellent reliever, had saved many games for the Phillies. Their hopes to win a pennant rested on his staying healthy.

"How did it happen?" she pursued.

"It was real fluky. Joey only threw a ball back to him on the mound."

"Joey?"

"Yeah. Dimitrio. He feels terrible." Hollister shook his head again. "I'm telling you, it's bad luck. I shouldn't have stepped on the foul line last night."

"Excuse me?"

"We never step on the foul lines when we go on or off the field," he explained.

Heather didn't believe in luck, good or bad. But she knew baseball players could be very superstitious. She suspected there was a more sinister reason for what was going on.

The game that night rattled everyone's nerves. The lead constantly volleyed back and forth, with first the Phillies, then the Cardinals seizing the advantage. Manager Danny Mastrodoni summoned Felix Undeljar from the bull pen to relief pitch in the top of the eight inning. The hurler insisted his hand felt well enough. It didn't stay that way. With no men out and the bases loaded, Undeljar struck out the first batter. Then the next one hit a bullet right back to the mound. The ball smashed against Undeljar's unprotected pitching hand. Felix collapsed in pain.

7

Basic Training

Heather watched the Phillies trainer and the manager help Undeljar to the clubhouse. Nearby the team's broadcasters speculated about the pitcher's injury and how it might affect the team's pennant chances. Although they felt grim about Undeljar, their common consensus was, "Thank God for Dimitrio!"

"What a shame," Dave Knox told Heather. "Felix has been the backbone of the relief squad. It's a good thing they got Dimitrio."

"He sure is in the right place at the right time," she said. *But there's something about Dimitrio's "heroic efforts" that disturbs me,* she thought.

When play resumed, the rookie reliever took to the mound. On the second pitch, the St. Louis batter hit a grounder to third. The Phillies turned it into an easy double play to end the inning. In the top of the ninth, Lefty Washington drove home two runs with a double, and the Phillies led by one point. Then Joe Dimitrio ended any hopes for a Cardinals come-back by striking out their last three hitters. The dugout emptied as his teammates rushed to congratulate Dimitrio.

"Heather!" John Krauss called out as she prepared to leave. "I have a surprise for you. How would you like to talk to Joe Dimitrio for as long as you like?" he asked eagerly. "I know the big boys keep bumping you."

"You know I would." Her heart pounded in anticipation. *This could be my chance to learn more about him!* she thought.

"Then follow me!" he said confidently.

The teenager hesitated. "Follow you where?"

"The players are going to a party at Bib Shoon's condo. If you come with me, I'll make sure Joe talks to you."

Something inside told Heather not to go. *Oh, but it is tempting,* she thought. *I'd really be on the "inside" if I went. I doubt that many reporters get invitations like this. I might even learn more about Kevin Shirley's odd behavior.*

In spite of the attractive offer, Heather declined. "My family came tonight, and they're waiting downstairs," she said honestly.

"I can take care of that! I can reassure the folks and promise to deliver you safely home," he grinned.

Heather disliked his arrogance. "Thanks anyway, John, but no. That's my decision," she said firmly and left the press box.

In the car on the drive back to Kirby, Heather told her parents and Jenn about Krauss's invitation and her response.

"Heather, I'm very proud of you," her mother smiled, leaning over the seat. "You showed good sense."

The teenager also caught her father's pleased expression in the rearview mirror.

"Thanks, Mom. It wasn't where I belonged."

"But what an offer!" Jenn exclaimed. "I would have been sorely tempted."

"I was," Heather admitted.

"So this John Krauss really seems to like you," Mr. Reed commented, maneuvering through heavy traffic on the Schuylkill Expressway.

"I'm afraid so," she sighed.

"Tell me if he becomes a nuisance," her dad instructed.

The following night Heather and Jenn went to a special youth group meeting at their church. The organization usually didn't gather on summer Sundays, but they had some special events to plan, including an outing to a Phillies game.

"I've already got the tickets," announced their youth minister, Dick Walker. "It's going to be a Friday 'group night.'"

"What date is that?" Amy Everett asked. Heather had recently helped Amy's family solve a mystery that involved a real-estate scam.*

Dick scanned his newsletter from the Phillies. "July 15th."

"Too bad," she mourned. "I thought we'd be free that day, but my dad needs to take his vacation that week."

"Isn't that the double-header game?" Jenn inquired.

"Uh-huh," Dick replied.

"That's the night Heather will be playing in the media game!" The redhead was beside herself.

---

* Read more about Amy's story in *The Toxic Secret*.

"What's this all about?" Dick showed a keen interest.

"The print reporters will play the broadcast media. I think it's great all of you will be there." She beamed.

"I do, too!" Dick smiled. "We'll cheer you on, Heather!"

When the gathering ended, Evan Templeton approached Heather. He had recently moved to town and played in the outfield for Kirby High's baseball team.

"I'm willing to give you some pointers," the cute brunette told her. "If you need them," he added hastily.

"I sure do!" she said. They discussed where to meet and when.

On the way home in Heather's car, Jenn expressed her excitement about Heather's upcoming dates with Evan.

"I'm not sure they're official dates," Heather countered. "We're just going to play ball."

"I saw the look in his eyes," Jenn teased. "I'm sure it said 'dates.'"

"Well, good!" Heather giggled. "I think Evan's really cool."

"He is. I wish things were better for me in the romance department," Jenn complained.

"Still pining for my brother, huh?" Heather teased as she steered the sedan toward home.

"I've waited so long for him to notice me that I can hang in there a bit longer," she sighed. "Meanwhile, Pete Gubrio asked if I'd sit with him at the Phillies game." He also belonged to their large youth group.

"I think that's terrific!" Heather exclaimed.

"I suppose. I just wish he were Brian."

Heather had two weeks to prepare for the media contest. With covering the Phillies games, writing her stories, going to youth group, and helping around the house, she stayed very busy. She and Evan got together three times, and he gave good pointers about playing baseball. He proved to be a patient and capable teacher.

"I think you're doing really well," he praised her after one session at the high school ball field. They were cooling off with frozen yogurt at the dairy palace.

"Thanks. I think you're a good instructor." Heather licked her chocolate cone then said, "My fielding's still pretty shaky, though."

"You hit well, and you run fast," Evan summarized. "Maybe you won't need to handle the ball much. If you play third base, you'll have the shortstop to help you."

"I think that's a good idea."

"Don't worry if you mess up a play," her friend encouraged. "It's just for fun, right?"

"Right. But I hate messing anything up," she admitted.

After a few quiet moments, Evan spoke again. "You know, Heather, I'd like to spend more time with you. You're so busy, though. And, well," he stammered, "with you around all those famous Phillies, I wonder if a high-school friend might be too boring." He couldn't bring himself to look directly at Heather.

"I'd enjoy doing things with you, too," she said. "I'm not too busy for that." Heather paused. "Ballplayers lead exciting lives, but they're made of the same stuff as everyone else. Anyway, I don't think it's what we do that makes us important. I think we're worth something because God made us."

Evan smiled broadly, and his clear blue eyes sparkled. "I'm really glad to hear that."

"I don't need to sit in the press box for the second game of that double-header we're going to," she told him.

"Then will you sit with me for the second game?" he asked hopefully.

"I'd love to!"

"I think he's a pleasant young man," her father approved after Evan brought Heather home.

"I agree," said Mrs. Reed. "Did you say he lived in the Philadelphia area before coming to Kirby?"

Heather nodded. "Yes. He lived in Haverford."

"I like Evan too," Brian chimed in. "Does he have an older sister?" he asked mischievously.

"Sorry, big brother," Heather teased. "He's an only child."

In the days leading up to the media game, Heather thought the tension at the ballpark had decreased. She believed it was due to a lull in the Kevin Shirley storm. Since the Players' Association ruled in Shirley's favor, Carl Day Springer hadn't pushed the issue further. However, the player remained aloof.

The Phillies were winning more games now behind the incredibly talented Joe Dimitrio. The reliever had chalked up eleven saves in his brief career with the Phillies. Something bothered Heather about Dimitrio, though. While he acted friendly toward all the other reporters, he usually just smiled at her and quickly walked away.

I wonder why? she asked herself. *Is it because of my reputation for solving mysteries? If so, what is he hiding? Of course, he would've talked to me at that party John Krauss invited me to. At least that's what John claimed. So why not at the stadium?* She couldn't figure it all out.

Krauss kept busy publicizing the Phillies Fun Fair, so he didn't badger Heather as much as usual. It looked like the event would be a great success for the team. Krauss put a good deal of effort into the TV and radio advertising, and Phillies fans snatched up the tickets. After just one week of sales, there were none left. Krauss, however, made sure Heather and her family had free passes.

"He definitely likes you," Jenn teased one afternoon.

"And I definitely dislike him. There's got to be a reason for the attention he showers on me," she sputtered.

"Any ideas?" her friend asked.

"Nothing firm, but I just don't trust him," Heather concluded.

When the Friday Group Night arrived, the youth club piled in the church bus and headed to Veterans Stadium. Heather sat with Evan, across the aisle from Jenn and Pete. Mr. and Mrs. Reed and the McLaughlins were there as chaperones, and Brian came, too. Sixty other people filled the bus and sang their way to the ball game. As they neared the stadium, the group's excitement rose to a fevered pitch for a totally different reason.

The bus suddenly stopped in bumper-to-bumper traffic as it began exiting the Schuylkill Expressway a few blocks from the stadium. Emergency sirens split the air, and fire trucks raced on the road beneath them toward the sports complex.

"What's going on?" everyone asked, craning their necks for a good look.

"The stadium's on fire!" Heather shouted.

8

Fired Up!

Heather made her way down the aisle of the bus to her parents and said excitedly, "Mom and Dad, I'd like to see what's going on."

"I'm not sure that's wise, Heather," Mrs. Reed hesitated. "There's such a commotion! It looks dangerous."

"We're only a half mile away. Traffic's at a stand-still, so I won't get run over," she pleaded her case.

Her father, a curious journalist in his own right, sat on the edge of his seat and peered out the window at the dense smoke. Then he exchanged a knowing look with his wife, and they nodded at each other.

"I'll go with you, Heather."

His daughter grabbed her bag with clothes for the media game and bade hasty good-byes to her companions.

"Be careful!" they cautioned her.

Mr. Reed quickly explained to Dick Walker what was going on. A short time later Heather and her dad were making their way through the throng at the stadium. As they got closer, Heather realized the fire wasn't as big as the smoke had first led her to believe. The thick smoke only made it seem like the whole stadium was burning.

"Dad, I think the fire's probably near the far side of the parking lot!" she shouted above the noise.

"I think you're right!" he called back.

They finally reached the press gate after a strenuous effort to slice through the mob. But a policeman on a chestnut horse prevented them from going inside.

"You can't go farther," he ordered.

When Patrick Reed and his daughter displayed their press credentials, however, the officer changed his tune. He impatiently waved them onward.

"Do you know what happened?" Heather shouted up to him.

"Car fire!" he hollered.

"What do you mean?" she pursued, but the policeman answered no further questions.

"I wonder what kind of car fire," Heather said to her father. "Let's try to find it!"

"I doubt we can get near the area," he remarked. "We'd better just go to the press gate."

"All right," she sighed.

A policewoman checked their documents at the gate; normally a Phillies official did that job.

"When did the fire start?" Heather asked her.

"A half hour ago."

"Do you know how?"

The woman shook her head. "I was on duty across the street when I saw the flames."

"Was there an explosion?"

"No," she replied.

"Was anyone in the car?" The teenager didn't think so because she hadn't seen any ambulances leave the area.

"No."

"Thank God," Mr. Reed murmured.

The officer hastened to add, "There were three cars involved, and they all belonged to ballplayers." Other reporters waited behind the Reeds to get through, so the policewoman ended the conversation. "Please step inside."

They thanked her and entered the press gate, where Public Relations Director Barry Webster answered some reporters' questions. Heather and her dad quickly moved closer to hear what he was saying.

"Well, you heard wrong, I'm afraid. Yes, they were players' cars, but no one was in them," he explained patiently. "Again, I don't know to whom they belonged. My assistant is questioning the Phillies in the clubhouse right now."

"What started the fire?" shouted one journalist.

"I don't know yet."

Heather wondered whether he did know and just wouldn't tell. *Another weird event,* she considered. *This smacks of foul play.*

"I suggest you come in and follow as normal a routine as possible," Webster told the newspeople. "The fire didn't spread, so the stadium's safe. We're creating a bottleneck, so come on through."

The sportswriters, most of them carrying gym bags for their game, hustled inside.

Her father's job as managing editor of *The Philadel-phia Journal* gave him access to the playing field and press box.

Heather proudly led him toward the dugout. She enjoyed having him see this place that was so important to her. Although no players were around, they did find *The Journal's* sports editor.

"Pat, good to see you!" Mr. Knox greeted Heather's father with a hearty handshake.

"Hi, Dave." They exchanged pleasantries, then Mr. Reed asked, "Do you know which players' cars caught fire?"

"Nope. The police and players are sorting through the rubble."

"What do you make of it, Mr. Knox?" asked Heather.

The big man's expression was grim. "Cars don't just burn."

"Maybe an irate fan did it," another reporter suggested.

"That's one possibility," Knox agreed.

Heather thought that sounded too simple.

Twenty minutes later Carl Day Springer met the press in a room near the clubhouse. Finding no place to sit, Heather, her dad, and Dave Knox leaned against a wall. The place quickly grew stuffy from jostling reporters and the strong lights of remote TV cameras.

The powerful owner motioned for silence and got it— immediately. Barry Webster, John Krauss, and Danny Mastrodoni flanked him. Dozens of cameras clicked into action making it difficult to hear when Springer began to talk.

"Please speak louder, sir!" someone yelled.

Springer raised his voice. "I have a brief statement to read," he said. "At approximately four o'clock this afternoon a fire started in the players' parking area. None of the Phillies were near their cars at the time. There were no injuries. The vehicles belonged to Joe Dimitrio, Bib Shoon, and Kevin Shirley." He spat out the last name. "Firefighters contained the blaze before it spread to other cars. The Philadelphia arson squad is investigating. I have no further comments at this time."

Several reporters shouted questions all at once, but Springer hastily exited through a side door to the locker room. Heather wanted to ask questions too, but stadium guards ordered the reporters to leave.

"I guess that's all we get for now," she sighed. "Either Mr. Springer knows more than he's telling us, or he doesn't have a handle on this himself yet."

Mr. Knox pursed his lips but didn't agree or disagree with his young friend. "I doubt the players will talk to us tonight," he concluded. "Pat, will you join us in the press box?"

"Yes, I believe I will. Do you mind Heather?"

"Not at all!" she exclaimed.

"Good. Maybe we can pick up some clues together." He winked knowingly at his daughter. "So, my young sleuth, what do you make of this?"

Heather smiled. "Carl Day didn't tell us how the fire began. Nor did he say—if it were an irate fan—why he or she destroyed two of the most popular Phillies' cars."

"Yes, Kevin Shirley I can understand. But not Joe Dimitrio or Bib Shoon. Of course," he continued, "this fan may have set fire to Shirley's car, and it spread," Mr. Reed surmised.

"That could have happened," Heather said. "But I'm open to other ideas because so many weird things have been happening to this ball club this season."

"Where does she get this from?" Knox elbowed Pat Reed playfully.

"My side of the family," he smiled sheepishly.

Heather wasn't the only person trying to work out the latest mystery. The press box buzzed with theories about what—or whom—caused the car fires. The Reeds heard every suggestion from a bomb to engine trouble.

"Maybe the Ol' Man figured this was the best way to get ride of Kevin Shirley," one sportswriter joked.

He may be right, Heather considered darkly. *Mr. Springer told me he doesn't have to play by the rules with Kevin.*

During the second inning, John Krauss came over to Heather and her dad. For once the teenager felt happy to see him. "Do you have news?" she asked eagerly.

"Nothing you don't already know," the shaggy-haired P.R. man replied.

"John Krauss, I'd like you to meet my father, Patrick Reed," Heather introduced.

Mr. Reed shook the young man's hand. "My daughter has told me all about you," he said.

"It's, uh, good to meet you, sir." Krauss suddenly lost some of his swagger.

"Isn't Heather amazing for a sixteen-year-old?" Mr. Reed stressed Heather's age on purpose.

"Yes, she certainly is," stuttered Krauss.

Heather stifled a giggle. Then she recovered enough to ask, "Do you think someone deliberately set the fire?"

"Around this club, I wouldn't doubt it." He sniffed. "Maybe Shirley did it to get back at the management."

"Why would he destroy his own car?" asked a surprised Mr. Reed.

Krauss spread his hands. "To make him look innocent?" he guessed. "I hear he's jealous of Joe Dimitrio. At any rate, the fire's keeping me busy. I'd better go. It was good to meet you, Mr. Reed."

"Same here."

When the public relations assistant left, Heather punched her dad lightly on the arm. "Really, Dad! You frightened him!"

"I meant to!" Then he grew sober. "What a strange suggestion he made!"

"Dad, I think he may be in league with Mr. Springer to make Kevin Shirley want to leave this team."

"You may be right," he consented. Mr. Reed shook his head back and forth. "With everything that's going on around here, just be careful."

"I will, Dad," she assured him.

The game seemed secondary to Heather that night. Not only did the fire command her attention, but anticipation for the media game filled her as well. When it finally came time to get ready, the teenager said good-bye to her dad and went to the ladies' room to change her clothes. Then she went to the home plate runway behind the field where other journalists waited. They took the field after the Phillies rallied in the bottom of the ninth inning to beat the Dodgers 5–3.

The media ball game was a lot of fun. Heather forgot the fire and other controversies and threw herself into the contest. She played third base for the print media and easily fielded the balls that came to her. Heather even initiated a double-play for two outs. *Evan's lessons really helped,* she thought, stepping up to bat. *Let's see if I can hit the ball now.*

The pitcher, a scruffy morning disc jockey, threw the ball right over the plate. Heather took a big swing at it, expecting to watch it soar down the third base line. When she did connect, however, her bat exploded!

9

Foul Play

The explosion's force sent Heather wheeling to the ground, pressing her hands against her ears. Her teammates rushed over with the Phillies doctor, Lee Kim, to see if she was badly hurt. Mr. Reed and Dick Knox had been watching the game from the enclosed area behind home plate. They, too, hurried onto the field.

"Can you hear me?" Dr. Kim asked.

"Yes, but my ears are ringing," said Heather.

"Do you feel pain anywhere?"

Heather sat up slowly and, seeing her father, managed a weak smile. "I don't have any pain, just the ringing in my ears."

Just then Mrs. Reed reached her daughter's side and started asking questions. In her concern for Heather, she forgot to present herself to the Phillies physician.

"Hey, lady," Dr. Kim protested, "I'm in charge here!"

"I'm Dr. Reed, Heather's mother," she explained hastily.

Then the two doctors worked together, making certain Heather was okay.

Except for the jolt from the exploding bat, Heather felt fine. The stadium guards retrieved pieces of the shattered bat and made a quick assessment. Someone had drilled a quarter-inch hole in the top of the bat and filled it with a small explosive device. Sometimes baseball players bored holes in their bats and put pieces of cork or rubber balls inside to make the bats hit better. Then they sealed the hole, smeared it with pine tar, and carved a wood grain pattern around it to cover their tracks. This was known as "corking a bat." As for fingerprints, the police on the scene said there were too many to tell anything conclusive.

"It was probably a practical joke," one of them said. "You know these baseball players."

"That was not funny. Help me get Heather off this field so we can examine her in privacy," her mother huffed.

The policemen quickly cleared a way through the worried bystanders. Heather walked with her father's help, and the crowd gave her a round of applause. The media game continued with a substitute for Heather at third base. Dr. Kim led the Reeds to his office near the Phillies' clubhouse. After a brief check-up, both physicians decided Heather did not require further treatment.

"Are you sure your ears are better?" her mother asked.

"Yes, Mom. The ringing isn't nearly as loud now."

"Would you like us to take you home?" her father asked.

"Not at all," she insisted. "I want to see the second game. I have a date, remember?"

Heather showered and put on her street clothes, then she and her parents went to their seats. On the way, Mr. Reed asked how she had selected her bat.

"It was in a crate the bat boys set out for us. I tested them all and chose the lightest one. The others were far too heavy for me." Her hazel eyes narrowed. "Someone might have wanted me to choose that bat over the others. I was the smallest player on either of the teams and, therefore, the most likely to use it."

"This is too much for the likes of me," sighed her mother. "First the fire, now this."

Heather didn't share the rest of her thoughts for fear her mother would forbid her to cover the Phillies. *That was no coincidence or innocent prank,* she reflected. *I wonder if Mr. Springer might want to scare me away? He may regret those threatening remarks he made to me about Kevin Shirley. Of course, if Kevin is trying to get back at the press for his troubles, he might've corked that bat.*

In spite of the explosion and her preoccupation with the mystery, Heather enjoyed being with her friends for the second game. Everyone in the group expressed relief that she was feeling well.

"We were really worried," Dick Walker spoke for them all. "What a night!"

An investigation by the Philadelphia Fire Department determined that the car fires were an act of arson. The police continued their search for the guilty party. They also decided someone had simply played a practical joke on the media by corking the bat. When questioned, the bat boy insisted he hadn't done the mischief. "I don't know who did it," he stated.

Everyone forgot the incident, except the teenage sleuth. She felt certain someone didn't want her around the team. *It's probably the same person causing the rest of the trouble,* she thought. She wanted to get to the bottom of the case before someone was seriously hurt.

Heather finally had an opportunity to talk to Joe Dimitrio on the last game of the home stand.

"Have you fully recovered from your accident with the bat?" he asked as she snapped on her tape recorder for the interview.

"Yes. Thank you for asking."

"I'm glad. I'll bet that really scared you!"

"You can say that again."

"Did you ever find out how that happened?"

Heather shook her head. "The police say it was a practical joke." *Why the interest?* she wondered.

"Baseball players are famous for those," he commented. "It's just that sometimes people get hurt."

"I guess. Anyway, I can hardly believe we caught up with each other. I started thinking you were avoiding me."

A shadow crossed the young player's face, but he quickly summoned his considerable charm. "Now, why would I do that? It just gets so crazy here before games." He smiled.

"It certainly does."

"So many reporters want interviews, and I did talk to you a little earlier. Sorry I took so long getting back to you."

"I understand," Heather remarked. "You're an overnight sensation, according to *The Journal*."

He blushed slightly. "I just hope I live up to the fans' expectations."

"So far you have. Weren't you nervous coming straight to the big time after just one season in the minor leagues?" Heather asked.

"I think getting called up to the Phillies surprised me so much I didn't have time for the jitters," he explained.

"What do you think is the biggest difference between playing for a minor league team and playing with the Phillies?"

"That's easy. The facilities are much better up here. You also get to fly to away games, rather than sit on chartered buses for hours on end. Then there are the big-name players up here, the ones on bubble gum cards. It's really exciting." He sounded "little boyish" in his enthusiasm.

"So you're glad it took such a short time for you to make it big?" Heather guessed.

"Sure I am," he answered. "But the minors are a good place to start."

"You just wouldn't want to spend your career there, right?" she teased.

The same shadowy look reappeared, and Dimitrio squirmed on the dugout bench.

"I get the impression you dislike talking about the minors," she said candidly.

Dimitrio looked startled but quickly recovered. "It's not my favorite subject."

Although Heather wondered why, she felt she had pushed far enough. "To what do you credit your amazing success?"

"Hard work," he said simply. Dimitrio glanced at his watch a bit impatiently.

"Are you busy?" Heather asked.

"Always."

"I just need a few more minutes," she told him. Dimitrio nodded for her to proceed. "How do you feel about entering games in tough situations?"

"I thrive on competition," he responded. "And I won't always be a relief pitcher."

Heather remembered her earlier conversation with the Phillies pitching coach. "Shifty thinks your one drawback is that you tire easily. Is there something you can do about that?"

"There sure is," he muttered.

"Like what?"

"Hey, a guy needs to keep some secrets!" he joked. "Listen, Heather, I've got to go."

The teenage reporter managed to get in just one more question. "I forget," she said. "Are you married?"

Dimitrio looked flustered. "Uh, no. See ya later, Heather!"

Why did he act like that? she mused, turning off the tape recorder. *He seemed real edgy about the minor leagues, and then to answer a question about marriage like that . . . he's got to be hiding something.*

The Phillies won their game that night, then went away for a week-and-a-half-long road trip to play West Coast teams. Heather spent the time writing articles for *The Kirby Courier.* She also met with Harper Richards to discuss ways to improve her skills. Although he hadn't seemed like a kindred spirit at first, Richards quickly became a friend, and the teenager's writing thrived under his guidance.

One afternoon Heather phoned the Phillies Public Relations Department to get further information about Joe Dimitrio's background. Even in other reporters' stories about the new star, she read mainly about baseball details and little on him. Barry Webster took her call.

"I have something more somewhere." Heather heard him shuffle papers on the other end. "He came up so quickly and made such a good first impression that we didn't have time to get more than the basics about Joey."

"His minor league statistics are in the media guide," Heather said, "but I want to know about him as a person."

"I gave him a fact sheet to fill out, but he hasn't returned it. He's been pretty busy," Webster hastened to explain. "On top of that, this Fun Fair's got us hopping. I'll try to get you something, though. Do you have a deadline?"

"The sooner the better," Heather replied.

Webster promised to see what he could do, and they hung up. *I may be right after all,* Heather thought. *Joe Dimitrio is hiding something. I'm going to call the Reading Phillies to see what personal information they have on him.*

She found the number in the media guide and asked for public relations. But they only had a secretary to answer her questions. Heather explained what she wanted, and the woman put her on hold while she checked her files.

"I'm afraid I can't find much either," the secretary said after several minutes.

"Is that unusual?" Heather asked.

"Maybe just a little," the woman answered. "It does happen sometimes."

Heather thanked her and hung up. *Something smells rotten in Veterans Stadium, and I think Joe Dimitrio may know what it is. In fact, he may be causing the stink and not Carl Day Springer—unless they're partners in this.*

She sighed. *All I have to go on is a hunch. I'll have to be keenly aware of anything that appears out of the ordinary with either of them. As for Kevin Shirley, he keeps so much to himself I only ever see him on the field during games. It's hard to know what he's up to.*

Heather went over to Jenn's to clear her mind for a while. As they lay sunning in the backyard listening to Jenn's radio, an announcer interrupted the music. "Well, folks, the Phillies have done it again, and I don't mean win! The San Diego Police have arrested pitcher Kenny Scribner!"

10

Arrested Development

Did you hear that?" shouted Heather. She leaned over and turned up the radio.

"I sure did!" Jenn cried.

"Late this morning the San Diego Police arrested Phillies pitcher Kenny Scribner for drug possession," the broadcaster said.

Jenn clapped a hand to her forehead. "What could possibly happen next?"

Heather felt deeply shocked. "Kenny's such a neat guy, clean-cut and honest. I can't imagine him doing—or selling—drugs."

"Another element to your mystery, eh?" Jenn quipped. "Better crank up your computer. I have a feeling your editor will want a story on this one."

"I think you're right. I'm going home to call Mr. Richards right away."

Jenn became thoughtful. "The pitching staff is really having a hard time, isn't it?"

Heather nodded. "I wonder why it's the pitchers?" Her look was faraway.

"Earth to Heather. Earth to Heather," Jenn called out. "Are you still going roller-skating tonight?" Their youth group had planned an outing at the local rink.

"I'll be there."

Heather quickly pulled on her sandals and raced across the yard to her house. Ella Freemont, the housekeeper, threw a broad hand up to block her entrance. "Stop right there!" she commanded. "I just waxed this floor."

"How about letting me in the front door?" The Reeds almost never used that entrance, but this counted as an emergency.

"I'll go open it for you." When Heather came inside, Mrs. Freemont asked, "What's going on, anyway?" The teenager quickly explained the situation, and the older woman retorted, "I think the Phillies ought to call this season quits. Nothing's going right for them."

Not if I have anything to do with it! Heather thought as she went to her bedroom. *I'll bet someone planted those drugs. Why Kenny, though? Is it because he's a pitcher?* She considered this angle more deeply. *First there was the so-called mix-up at the hospital involving Mike Clausen's father, and that threw off Mike's game. Then Felix Undeljar got hurt "accidentally." And those cars caught fire, including Joe Dimitrio's. After that, Felix was reinjured. Now there's this mess with Kenny. Why Phillies' pitchers?*

Heather called Harper Richards to find out if he wanted her to do the story for *The Courier*.

"I've heard all about Scribner," the editor remarked. "I called the Phillies and found out Carl Day Springer will give a press conference in two hours. Can you be there?"

"I'll let you know in about five minutes," she promised.

Heather phoned her dad at his office asking permission to take the car to Veterans Stadium. That morning Brian had biked to his landscaping job, leaving behind the red sedan. Plus Mr. Reed had taken the train to work.

"All right," he consented. "You can pick me up afterward, and we'll come home together. Your mother's been at the hospital all day, so we can get some Chinese food on the way home."

"Thanks, Dad!" she said. Heather called her editor right back to say she would be at the press conference.

At the stadium reporters jammed a large room on the first level, waiting impatiently for the contentious owner. Heather asked Dave Knox if Carl Day Springer usually handled the press. "I thought that was public relations' territory," she commented.

"Not on this team," he grunted. "The Ol' Man tries to run the whole show."

The "Ol' Man" was not in a good mood. He strode into the room like a roaring lion looking for someone to devour. Tape recorders and TV cameras flicked on, creating a deafening noise and lights that made the place as bright as high noon.

"Do you think Kenny Scribner is innocent?" Heather called out.

Springer became sarcastic. "You boys—and girls—probably want me to make apologies for Scribner's behavior. Well, I won't do it. This team has enough trouble with players who don't concentrate on baseball. And the buck stops here!" He pounded the lectern for emphasis. "What

I want," he struck his fist again, "is a team full of players like Joe Dimitrio. That rookie has more finesse in his wallet than some of these guys have in their huge bank accounts." He ranted on about greed and corruption and his longing for the good old days of baseball. This lasted twenty minutes.

"What's the underlying cause of the team's problems?" a TV sportscaster asked.

"Laziness!" Springer bellowed. "These guys draw fat salaries, then sit on their duffs."

"Sir," a female reporter yelled, "have you and Kevin Shirley reached a compromise? We haven't heard much about him lately."

The owner growled, "I never compromise."

"Would you explain?" she followed up.

"There are changes in the works," he answered obscurely, refusing to elaborate.

Public Relations Director Barry Webster took the microphone. He said, "I'd like to add that Kenny Scribner submitted a request for an administrative leave. That's pending the outcome of an investigation by the Commissioner's office."

Heather had a lot to consider on the way to pick up her dad. *I wish we could've heard Kenny's side of the story,* she thought. *I believe someone framed him. But who? I wonder if Mr. Springer is trying to clean house and get rid of the players he considers lazy. He said changes are in the works.*

The next day at the ball park, John Krauss told Heather that Springer had ordered an intense advertising blitz to promote the Phillies Fun Fair. "It's going to be some campaign!" he said enthusiastically.

"But you've already sold out of tickets," the teenager responded.

"True. We're going to establish phone lines. People who can't come can call in pledges for the hospital. The idea is to saturate Philadelphia with good feelings about the team. Get their minds off the likes of Kenny Scribner and Kevin Shirley," he said in disgust. "Did you see the first commercial? We shot it a week ago, and it ran last night."

In the ad, patients from Children's Medical Center surrounded Joe Dimitrio. He said cheerfully, "Help us help the Delaware Valley's children!"

"Yes, I did," she said. "I liked it a lot, but why did you use Joe? He's so new to the team."

"The fans adore him," Krauss gushed. "I was wondering, Heather, can I get you to do a write-up about the fair for your paper?"

"I'll ask my editor," she replied. "It shouldn't be a problem, though." In the back of her mind, Heather grew more suspicious about both John Krauss and his buddy, Joe Dimitrio. *Why does John constantly talk down other players and talk up Joe?* she wondered.

The public relations assistant was still chattering. "I'm also asking print and broadcast journalists if they'll run some rides and work the booths at the fair. Are you interested?"

"Uh, sure," Heather said. "What would I be doing?"

"Let's see." He consulted a list on a clipboard. "I'd like to put you at the dunking booth. The players will take turns getting dunked, and we need someone to hand them towels."

"Sounds good to me." Heather took the opportunity to see if Krauss would do *her* a favor. "By the way, John, I'm having trouble finding background material on Joe Dimitrio. He doesn't like to talk about his past. I checked his minor league team, but they didn't have much to offer either. As you said, he's popular, and fans want to know more about him."

John Krauss's cool exterior melted ever so slightly. "I'll see what I can do." He consulted his watch and gave a phony sigh. "I'll be late for an appointment if I don't rush."

Heather felt suspicious. *So he has a secret, too!* she thought darkly.

In the morning Harper Richards said Heather could write about the Fun Fair for *The Courier.* "I'd like you to interview the players' wives, since they'll be putting it on. I think our readers would like to know who they are and what they're like."

Heather went to the stadium that hot afternoon to talk to some spouses. The team was on a road trip, and the Vet was starting to look like an old-fashioned carnival with a ferris wheel, games of chance, and kiddie rides. Talking to the wives proved interesting and fun. Heather obtained five interviews. When she approached Kevin Shirley's wife, the woman would not speak with her.

"It's nothing personal," she stated. "It's just that I don't think it would be wise, given the circumstances."

"I appreciate your honesty," Heather smiled. "I wish you well."

The woman looked more closely at the teenager. "Kevin has mentioned you," she said mysteriously.

"Me?" Heather gasped. "I didn't realize he knew I was alive!"

"Well, he does." Then Mrs. Shirley hurried away to her chores.

How do you like that? Heather thought. *Did she mean that as a threat—or maybe a warning?*

Heather felt distracted. She took a break and went to a booth for a drink. An attractive woman in her mid thirties was pouring lemonade there. Heather accepted a plastic cup of the ice-cold beverage and quickly drained it. She hadn't realized until then how thirsty the heat had made her.

"Thank you," she told the woman. "That was so good."

"Would you like another one?"

"Sure," Heather replied. "Are you a player's wife?"

"I'm a fiancée," she corrected.

"Whose?"

"Joe Dimitrio's," came the startling response.

11

Funny Feelings

The news startled Heather. The woman before her looked like she was well into her thirties. But Joe Dimitrio was only twenty-four! *I realize people with big age differences get involved with each other,* she reasoned. *But in this case, I'm suspicious. Could this be what Joe is trying to hide? If he loves her, though, why would Joe be ashamed of his fiancée's age? Maybe I can learn more about Joe through her!*

"I'm really glad to meet you," the teenager said eagerly. "I'm Heather Reed from *The Kirby Courier.* I've been working on a story about Joe's career."

"Is that right?" she asked nervously.

Heather noticed her uneasiness at once. She glanced around and, seeing that no one needed lemonade, pressed forward. "Is it okay if I ask you a few questions? I've found so little on your fiancée in the media guide and score card magazine. Then he's so busy, it's hard to track him down."

"I guess," she mumbled unenthusiastically.

The woman obviously didn't want to talk, and Heather wanted even more to get something about Joe out of her. "What's your name?" she began.

"Lynda."

"Lynda what?" Heather smiled a little at her tight-lipped response.

Her face reddened. "Ellis."

"I'm glad to meet you, Lynda Ellis."

The attractive brunette nodded impatiently. She looked as though she would rather be anywhere else.

"When do you plan to get married?"

"We haven't set a date," she said quickly.

"Have you known each other long?"

A simple question, but Lynda Ellis looked like she found it painful. "Fairly long. Listen, I need to get more lemonade." The pitcher was nearly full.

Heather was sure Lynda's jitters implied something important, but she couldn't force the woman to talk. With regret the young reporter thanked Lynda for the drink and her time.

"You're welcome," came the response. "I'm sorry I can't help you more."

That was so weird, Heather considered as she walked away. *Why wouldn't Lynda answer those basic questions? I wasn't trying to trick her! Come to think of it, Joe hesitated on the marriage question too. Why? And what's this with their age difference? I wonder whether the great Joe Dimitrio, savior of the Phillies, is all he's cracked up to be?*

Contrary to Lynda Ellis, the other players' wives and fiancées spoke eagerly to Heather. They admitted that the current season challenged them, but they were still glad their men played for the Phillies. The only thing they wouldn't discuss was the disasters that had befallen the team.

As she made the rounds, Heather noticed Lynda Ellis kept to herself. *I know!* the teenager thought. *I'll ask the next player's wife how well she knows Lynda.*

Her next interview was with catcher Pete Talarri's talkative wife. "I was wondering, Sarah, have you gotten to know Joe Dimitrio and his fiancée?" Heather inquired after several minutes.

The bright-eyed, sturdy-looking woman sniffed in disapproval. "No, but believe me, it hasn't been for lack of trying." She lowered her considerably loud voice and said confidentially, "Lynda doesn't act like she wants to be around us. We invite her to our get-togethers, but she just snubs us. I'm surprised she's here today."

"Do you know anything about her at all?"

Sarah Talarri shrugged. "Nope! Why the interest?"

"I'm doing research on Joe Dimitrio for a story and can't find much about him," she explained.

"If you ask me, Heather, they're a couple of odd birds," Sarah concluded.

The three other women she spoke to told Heather almost the same thing about Lynda Ellis and Joe Dimitrio. *Now I know something's up with them,* she decided. *It's going to be tough uncovering their mystery.*

Two nights later the Phillies flew back to town for the Fun Fair. All the difficulties of the road trip faded as happy, jostling fans elbowed their way inside Veterans Stadium for the charity event. As part of Heather's article on the fair, Harper Richards had instructed her to ask people what they thought of the Phillies. In spite of the team's problems, the fans responded positively.

After conducting the informal survey, Heather found her parents and Jenn. They spoke for a few minutes before she reported to the dunking booth.

"Isn't this exciting?" Jenn squealed. "I got Mike Clausen's autograph!"

"Good for you!" Heather said.

"I doubt Kevin Shirley will show," Brian remarked cynically.

"I haven't heard anything either way. But I doubt it too. Why is that important to you?"

"I think it might help improve his image, if it isn't already beyond repair," her brother expressed. "I guess I'm just disappointed that someone I looked up to as a kid turned out so poorly after all."

"I know," his sister agreed. "Well, I'd better go. Be sure to stop by the dunking booth!"

"We wouldn't miss it!" her mother smiled.

Heather waved good-bye and went to her position near what was normally third base. A long line had already formed. Dave Knox invited people to "step right up." He sounded just like a carnival barker! When he noticed Heather, he took a few minutes away from the microphone to explain her job.

"You're in for a big surprise," he winked.

Heather's hazel eyes brightened. "What is it?"

"You'll see," he teased.

They assumed their positions, and Heather waited impatiently to learn about the surprise, hoping it had something to do with the mystery. She learned what it was when the first Phillie entered the dunking booth. *It was Kevin Shirley!* He smiled sheepishly at Heather with her open-mouthed stare. Then the big leaguer took the microphone from Dave Knox. The crowd gave a collective gasp at his unexpected appearance.

"I can only imagine what you're thinking," grinned Shirley. "It's just that the media have been taking shots at me all summer. I figured the fans deserved a few chances as well."

The people loved it. Loud whistles, cheers, and applause resulted. Kevin Shirley climbed up to the bench that would give way the minute someone struck the dunking device. He looked more like himself than he had all season.

"That man has class," Dave Knox told Heather quietly before he started announcing the action. "It's so good to have him back."

Heather nodded in agreement as her mind reeled. *I wonder what this means,* she thought. Then she grabbed a pile of thick towels and took up her post next to the dunking platform.

One by one fans paid to throw baseballs at the red dunking mechanism. Most of them missed, but a few found their mark, sending Kevin Shirley into the Plexiglas tank.

He was enjoying himself enormously and looked completely at ease. When Shirley left the booth to make way for other players, a few teenagers reluctantly approached him with baseballs they wanted signed. The third baseman didn't hesitate to fulfill their requests.

The Fun Fair proved a huge success for Children's Medical Center and the Phillies. Carl Day Springer appeared at the end, displaying a check for $500,000 made out to the hospital. The fans cheered wildly.

A little later, as Heather searched the crowd for her family and Jenn, Kevin Shirley walked up to her. "I'd like to talk to you," he said seriously.

"Me?" His request totally surprised her.

"Let's go to the dugout." He gestured toward it with his head.

"Sure," Heather stuttered. Part of her couldn't help wondering whether this were a trap of some kind. Shirley looked tense.

They walked quickly to the dugout where the All-Star waved off several sportswriters who gathered around him. They, too, were bursting with curiosity.

"I only want to talk to *her*," he told them firmly. The men and women stared at Heather in bewilderment and turned away disappointed.

"What's going on?" she asked after the others left. Heather was glad they sat in full view of the busy field where she could make a run for it if necessary.

"My wife, Connie, wants me to break my silence with the press. She thinks it would be best if people knew the truth about me."

Heather's heart pounded in anticipation. *This sounds like a confession!* she thought excitedly.

"I decided to tell you my story because Connie thinks you'll give me a fair hearing."

"I'll do my best," Heather said solemnly.

"I know it may seem strange to give this interview to a weekly paper, but after all that's happened, it'll help me work up the courage to face the big dailies. Besides, I'd like to think that someone might help my kid out someday by giving him a break."

The Phillies' third baseman swallowed hard, realizing how difficult this was going to be for him. "The public seems to have me all figured out. But they really don't have any idea what's going on," he explained. "Still I feel funny making something terribly personal so open for all the world to know. I've never cared for the attention I get as a ballplayer. This year it's been unbearable, and I never meant for that to happen at all. I just wanted to keep to myself."

Heather sat on the edge of the bench waiting for Kevin's revelation to unfold.

He stared off into the distance as stadium workers dismantled the Fun Fair. "We got some bad news at the beginning of spring training." The infielder's lips quivered slightly. "Our four-year-old son has leukemia."

12

Not As They Seem

Shirley swallowed hard again and bit his lower lip. He was on the verge of tears. Heather found a lump forming in her throat. She had expected to hear something totally different.

"When I saw those children with cystic fibrosis who wanted my autograph," he resumed, "I saw my son. I—," Shirley faltered. A few seconds later he said, "I couldn't do it." Tears filled his brown eyes, and he looked away.

Heather tried filling in other blanks. "I guess any charitable work would be emotionally draining for you. Is that why you've kept your distance?" He nodded. "I don't blame you, Kevin." She laughed slightly. "You really had me worried there for a while."

"How do you mean?" The player looked puzzled.

"Here I thought you might be so angry with the club you were behind all the team's mishaps," Heather explained.

"I'll bet it crossed many people's minds."

"Do you have any idea where all that's coming from?"

Shirley shook his head back and forth. "I've been in my little world, except for the car fire. Then I figured some irate fan wanted to teach me a lesson."

Heather was now certain of his innocence. Carl Day Springer, John Krauss, and Joe Dimitrio were more suspect in her mind than ever. After a few moments she asked, "How is your son?"

"Adam's taking treatments now, and he has a good attitude."

"I think his father does too," she responded kindly.

"Thanks, Heather. It was tough knowing what I knew and having people think ill of me—for the wrong reasons, especially Mr. Springer. He really hates me now."

"I have a feeling he'll change his mind when he hears the truth."

"I hope so. Go ahead and write the story. I won't give further interviews until you do."

"Thanks. I'll handle this as sensitively as I know how. You know, Kevin, I wouldn't worry what other people think," she advised. "Being at peace with your motives is what really matters."

"I appreciate that, Heather."

"I wish your family the best," she said, getting up to leave. "I'll pray for Adam's recovery."

"That means a lot. I've even started praying since this happened."

When Heather got home that night, she went to her room and mulled over the surprising events. She hadn't told her family or Jenn about what Kevin Shirley had said.

Although, she had felt tempted, when Brian said that he couldn't get over the player's presence at the Fun Fair.

I don't mistrust them, Heather thought. *But this is Kevin's story. I don't feel it's mine to share—except for the article. I should get to the bottom of the mystery soon. If Carl Day Springer has upset the team because he's angry with Kevin—and if he has an ounce of compassion—he'll stop these antics. If John Krauss and Joe Dimitrio are part of Springer's conspiracy, they'll settle down too. But if the owner's innocent, and Krauss and Dimitrio weren't in league with him, something else is going on,* she concluded.

Heather's sensitively written story about Kevin Shirley appeared two days later in *The Kirby Courier.* Her editor praised her lavishly for it. Her father said Heather would make a fine journalist if she chose that career path. The other sportswriters covering the Phillies treated her with more respect. Kevin himself thanked her in a handwritten note, and more players let her interview them. Only Joe Dimitrio kept his usual distance.

"Nice job," John Krauss told her at the stadium. But he sounded insincere.

"Thanks," Heather replied. "By the way, did you ever get me more information about Joe Dimitrio?"

The public relations assistant thumped his palm against his broad forehead. "I completely forgot!" he exclaimed. "I've been so busy these past few weeks with the Fun Fair. Sorry, Heather."

Heather didn't think he looked sorry at all. "When can you get it for me?" she persisted.

"Give me another week. A lot can happen in that time," he answered vaguely.

After Krauss left, Heather sat in the dugout, thinking. *I'll do a little of my own investigating,* she determined. *Krauss, Joe, and Lynda are definitely up to something.*

The next day the teenage detective again looked up Dimitrio in the media guide. *I'll bet he pitched for the high school team,* she decided. *If I call his school, they can probably tell me something about Joe. I think he's from somewhere in Ohio.*

The guide confirmed that Dimitrio hailed from Columbia in that state. Heather called the town's high school, and the principal's secretary answered. The teenage reporter asked if she knew anything about a former student named Joe Dimitrio who now played baseball for the Philadelphia Phillies.

"Joe, what-did-you-say-his-last-name-was?" the woman inquired.

"D-i-m-i-t-r-i-o."

"I don't recognize that name, and I've been here twenty-two years. When did he graduate?"

Heather made a quick calculation. "He's twenty-four, so I'd say six or seven years ago."

The secretary entered the information in her computer, clucking her tongue constantly as she worked. Finally she reported, "I'm sorry, but I have no record of anyone named Joseph Dimitrio."

"Are you sure?" Heather persevered.

"Of course I am," the woman said testily.

"Thank you for your help." *Now that's strange,* Heather decided. *I wonder why they don't have an account of his high school days?*

Next she called Barry Community College, which the media guide also said Dimitrio had attended. The school's registrar told Heather that Joe Dimitrio had not gone to school there, nor had she ever heard of him.

The teenager felt totally baffled. *Why would Joe say he went to those schools when he didn't?*

Just then the phone rang, and Jenn was on the other end of the line. "Mom, Amy, and I are going out to Franklin Mills Mall," she announced. "Amy's up from Cape May today, and my brothers went to day camp, so it's just us girls. Want to come along?"

"Sure," Heather responded. "It will do me good to clear my mind."

"Still working on the Phillies' mystery?"

"Yes."

"I thought that ended when Kevin Shirley told you his story," Jenn reflected.

"That just opened a new chapter," her friend sighed.

An hour-and-a-half later Heather was at the sprawling outlet mall in northeast Philadelphia. Mrs. McLaughlin and Amy wanted to look for shoes, and Heather and Jenn were after jeans. The foursome agreed to meet at the food court in an hour.

The sixteen-year-olds went to three stores, but they didn't care for their selections or prices, so they headed to yet another. There they discovered aisles of fashionable—

and affordable—denims. Heather, however, found much more than jeans.

As she rummaged through a rack, she swept a row of jeans to one side to get a better look at her size. In doing so Heather rammed right into another customer.

"Please excuse me," she apologized. "I got careless and didn't see you."

"That's all . . ." the shopper's voice trailed off as she recognized the honey-brown-haired teen.

"Lynda Ellis!" Heather exclaimed.

Joe Dimitrio's fiancée became agitated. "Hello," she said hastily.

The tense look Heather had noticed at the stadium returned. Jenn looked up from her rack a few aisles away and came over to see what was going on.

"Lynda, this is my girlfriend, Jenn McLaughlin. Jenn, Lynda Ellis—Joe Dimitrio's fiancée."

"I'm very glad to meet you!" Jenn gushed. "I just love Joe!" Thinking that might not be the best thing to say about a woman's fiancé, she corrected herself. "I mean, I think he's terrific."

The first sign of a smile formed on the pretty woman's lips. Then she gazed intently at Heather. The teen waited expectantly for Lynda to say what was on her mind.

"I'm glad you admire Joe," she finally spoke. "And I hope you find what you're looking for," she told Heather mysteriously. "I must be going now."

Lynda Ellis quickly slid past them and out the store's entrance.

"I think that was bizarre," Jenn remarked.

Heather was about to respond when her right foot kicked at something on the floor. Bending down she saw and picked up a brown leather wallet.

"Someone dropped this," she commented. Heather opened it up and cried out, "It's Lynda Ellis's! I'm going after her."

On the way out of the store she glanced at the driver's license inside. It read, "Lynda K. Ellis." Next to age it said, "35." *She is a lot older than Joe!* Heather thought.

Lynda walked quickly through the crowded mall to the exit. By the time Heather reached the doors, the woman was gone. Heather went out into the hot afternoon sun and spotted her a few rows away, looking for her car.

"Lynda!" she yelled. "Lynda!"

The woman turned around and saw Heather waving her wallet. Lynda put a hand to her chest in relief; she hadn't even realized the object was missing. Heather ran up to her, panting. "I'm so glad I found you. You dropped this in the jeans store."

Lynda accepted the leather wallet and thanked Heather genuinely. "I really appreciate this. It was very nice of you." She looked at the girl searchingly.

"Is there something you want to tell me, Lynda?" Heather asked delicately.

The brunette inhaled deeply. "I wish . . ." she began, then stopped. "Let's just say things aren't always what they seem." With that she hopped into the car and drove away.

13

Strike One

Heather walked slowly back to the mall, deep in thought. *What did Lynda mean by, "Things aren't always what they seem?"*

"Did you catch her?" asked Jenn when Heather returned to the jean shop.

"Yes, and it was the weirdest thing!" She told her friend what had transpired.

"What do you think it means?"

"I haven't a clue right now," Heather admitted. "Still, I have a hunch something's about to give."

The next night at the stadium her suspicions concerning Joe Dimitrio and John Krauss deepened when the latter passed her by without so much as a nod. *What's with him?* she wondered. The P.R. assistant wore a tense expression.

Then Phil Hollister came over, bringing comic relief. "If it isn't Heather Reed, teenage sportswriter! How ya doin'?" He playfully slapped her on the back.

"Fine," she responded. Then she wrinkled her nose. "What is that dreadful odor?"

He grinned apologetically. "I don't exactly come up smelling like roses," he laughed. "That, my friend, is my socks."

Heather peaked at the once-white objects. "I take it you haven't changed them in a while?"

The handsome player smiled. "Since I've worn these babies, the team has won three games, and I've had a triple and five singles." He leaned closer. "Better avoid Clausen. He's had on the same warm-up shirt for two weeks."

Heather grimaced. "How do you guys stand it?"

Hollister shrugged. "If it wins games . . . "

"Do you really believe that?"

"Sure. That's baseball!"

Heather decided to write a story about superstitions among baseball players and asked Phil to help her.

"I'd love to!" he exclaimed. "I think that would make a fun piece."

First he told Heather that players don't get haircuts on game days. "It goes back to the Bible," Hollister explained. "When Samson got his hair cut, he lost his strength."

Among other superstitious quirks, he said ballplayers don't step on the field's foul lines as they go on or off.

"Why not?" Heather asked.

"Beats me! It's like 'step on a crack, break your mother's back!'"

After the fascinating talk, Heather mulled over recent events as she absently watched two new Phillies do a taped interview with a TV sportscaster. The management had replaced Kenny Scribner and Felix Undeljar with these minor league prospects. They didn't seem nearly as promising as Joe Dimitrio, but in that day's *Journal*, Danny Mastrodoni said the new hurlers would do temporarily.

Amazingly, even without Scribner and Undeljar's services, the Phillies had started winning. The team was now within three games of first place. This was largely due to Dimitrio's sensational pitching and the enthusiastic way he kept up the other players' spirits. In spite of the reliever's glowing reputation, however, his fiancée's words rang in Heather's ears: "Things aren't always what they seem."

Another major reason for the Phillies' turnaround was Kevin Shirley's return to the team's good graces. When Heather's story appeared about the player's son, Carl Day Springer invited the third baseman to his office where they enjoyed a heartfelt reunion.

"The whole thing was an unfortunate misunderstanding, and I'm sorry for my part in it," said Springer's astonishing press release the day after Heather's article came out. "I have promised the Shirleys their little boy will have the best doctor in the country at their disposal. I will do everything in my power to help them."

That gesture convinced Heather that the Phillies owner, outlandish though he could be, was more bark than bite. *There's something else going on here,* she concluded. *I'm pretty sure Krauss and Dimitrio are at the heart of it. It's odd, too—both have so much going for them, especially Joe. He's the darling of the Phillies! Why would he try to ruin the team?*

A one-sided argument startled the teenager out of her reflections. At the end of the dugout one of the phone cords stretched around the side going into the hall. Heather couldn't see the person who was yelling, but she strained to hear what he said.

"That's not what I meant!" the man cried out. "I'll take care of her!"

Could he possibly mean me? Heather gulped, feeling a little dizzy. Then she saw an arm reach around the corner and hang up the phone. All she could make out were the first three letters on the back of his practice jersey—D-i-m."

Joe Dimitrio! her heart pounded. *Who was he talking to? He sounded so different from usual. It was like hearing another person.*

When dugout attendant Dick Monnia came by a few minutes later, Heather asked him about the two phones. He explained that one was hooked up to the bull pen, and the other one, to the press box. Then Monnia pointed out which phone was which.

Dimitrio had been talking to someone in the press box, John Krauss maybe? Heather thought about how distracted Krauss had behaved earlier. *I'd better be careful,* she decided.

The following night Heather stayed home. Her parents had invited a couple of their friends to dinner, and they wanted Heather and Brian to be there. During the meal, the subject of the Phillies came up, and Mrs. Mimosa, an insurance agent, mentioned the recent car fires at Veterans Stadium.

"My company handled two of the claims," she mentioned. "And what claims! Those ballplayers drive expensive cars."

Heather became deeply interested. "They all have the same insurance company?"

"Most of them. We provide discounted rates in exchange for using their names in our advertising," the black woman explained.

"You said your company handled two of the claims," Heather mentioned. "Which player's didn't you process?"

"I'm not much of a fan to remember their names," Mrs. Mimosa apologized. "Let me think."

"The three were Bib Shoon, Joe Dimitrio, and Kevin Shirley." Heather tried to jog her memory.

"We didn't deal with Dimitrio."

"Do you know which company did?" she pursued.

"No."

"Could you find out?"

"Heather, don't interrogate our guests," Brian rebuked.

"It's all right," Mrs. Mimosa said kindly. "Call me tomorrow. I'm sure I can get that information."

Heather waited impatiently for a decent hour to contact her parents' friend the next day. She knew 7:30 was too early, so she went for a walk and tried to eat breakfast afterward. At 9:00 A.M. sharp she grabbed the phone. But Mrs. Mimosa told her to call back at 9:45; she had just come into the office.

"Your ballplayer's agent was Ray Bennett," the woman informed her then. "He owns a small business in New Jersey. Would you like his number?"

Heather eagerly wrote it, thanked Mrs. Mimosa, and called Bennett. "Are you the insurance man who handled the claim for Joe Dimitrio's car?"

"Who?" the agent asked.

"Joe Dimitrio of the Philadelphia Phillies."

"No," he said curtly.

Heather tried a different tactic. "His car caught fire and burned in Philadelphia a few weeks ago."

"Oh, yeah. Now I remember. Why do you want to know?"

"Bernice Mimosa, a friend who works for your company in Philadelphia, thought you could help me," she said lamely. Heather knew she was prying, and the man didn't have to give her the information.

"Well, all right. Let me check my computer." Several seconds later he reported, "Mrs. Lynda Ellis filed that claim."

Mrs! Heather couldn't believe it. "Was there any other name on the policy?"

"Yes, but not the guy you mentioned," he remarked. "Her beneficiary is her husband, Joe Ellis."

Heather dropped the phone.

14

Foul Ball

*E*ither *Lynda Ellis is engaged to Joe Dimitrio while married to a man named Joe Ellis, or Joe Dimitrio is lying about his identity,* Heather determined. She sat in deep thought on the comfortable rocking chair in her room. *What would motivate a great pitcher like Joe Dimitrio to lie about himself and undermine his teammates?*

Then she remembered two critical clues: his and Lynda's age difference and that most of the sidelined ballplayers had been pitchers. *I think I figured it out!* she thought excitedly. *Joe Dimitrio-Ellis isn't really twenty-four years old. He's a youthful-looking man, but not twenty-four. Somehow he broke into the major leagues with an assumed identity. To make a good impression on the Phillies, he paved the way by subverting his fellow pitchers. That made him look even better than he already is and secured his place on the roster. John Krauss is likely helping him carry out his plots because Joe promised a big reward in return, maybe money. I can see how Krauss might have arranged the fake call to Mike Clausen about*

*his father's supposed accident. Then he didn't give Mike
the hospital's message that there had been a mistake.*

Although Heather felt pleased with her theories, she
was far from satisfied. The teenager still didn't know
where Dimitrio came from or who he really was. She
intended to find out.

Heather's first move was a trip to Reading to question
Dimitrio's minor league team about him. She went to her
mother's basement-level office for permission to go. Mrs.
Reed was busy with her young patients, but she took a
short break to listen to Heather's request.

"You may go if you take someone with you. How
about Jenn?" she suggested.

When Jenn and Heather got to the modest Reading
Phillies stadium, Heather ended up talking to pitching
coach Wally Maxwell.

The young reporter explained that she was research-
ing an article on Joe Dimitrio. "How did you select Joe
to go up to the big leagues?" she asked.

The balding man basked in Dimitrio's success. "He was
dynamite down here. Tore up the hitters with that fast
ball. I knew we wouldn't keep him down here long."

"Would you say he was a natural? I ask that because
he spent so little time preparing for the majors," Heather
explained as Jenn listened quietly.

"You bet! A guy like him doesn't come around too
often. Never in all my days did I see a player that young
with as polished a technique as Dimitrio's. That usually

takes time. Anyway," he shook his head as if emerging from a fog, "when the Phillies needed pitching help fast, I didn't hesitate to recommend Joey."

"How did that process work?"

"Their roving scout came out here and got a good look at him. Joe really impressed the guy." Wally Maxwell grinned like the cat that swallowed the mouse. "Looks like I was right."

"There's one more thing, Mr. Maxwell," Heather asked. "Do you know if Joe came straight here after college?"

The coach frowned. "He could have. I don't recollect."

"Do you know if he's married?"

"Didn't you check the media guide?"

Heather avoided the question. "I just wondered if you ever met his wife."

"Well, he kept a pretty woman nearby, a brunette I believe."

"Thank you for your time," Heather said, rising.

"You're welcome."

On the way home, Heather said, "Mr. Maxwell told us how polished Joe Dimitrio is for his age. Jenn, I get the impression that he's been around for a long time."

"But there isn't any record of that," she protested.

"I'll bet there is." Heather's eyes looked dreamy. "Let's check the library for a book on major league ballplayers."

Neither the Kirby Public Library nor the Kirby College Library had such a book. Knowing the Phillies' archives would, Heather asked her mother if she and Jenn could go to the stadium.

"I need to be there anyway for tonight's game," she said.

"That's okay with me," Mrs. Reed approved.

"I know!" Jenn exclaimed. "Maybe we could visit Amy at the shore afterward. We can go after the game and stay overnight."

"I think that's a lovely idea, Jenn," said Mrs. Reed. "Heather needs to get her mind on something besides the Phillies! Give your mother and Amy a call to see if they approve."

Jenn used the phone to arrange their plans. Then Heather called Barry Webster and asked if Jenn could come along to the executive offices while she used the archives.

"Sure," he agreed. "She can even have dinner with you in the press dining club, and I'll leave a ticket for the game."

The girls quickly packed their overnight bags and drove to the Vet.

The "archives" were actually books, notebooks, and assorted files in bookcases that line a wall in the outer public relations office. Barry Webster had private quarters, but three underlings shared this room, including John Krauss. He kept trying to be of service, but Heather insisted she didn't need it.

"What are you looking for?" he inquired.

"Player statistics," she said vaguely. Heather knew he could locate the information she desired in a minute, but she couldn't risk that. The teens did their best not to look frustrated with their slow research; they didn't want him to insist on "helping" them.

When he finally left the room, Heather glanced at Krauss's desk and found exactly what she had been looking for—a massive baseball encyclopedia! She walked casually over to the volume and looked up "Joe Ellis." And she found him! When Jenn looked over her friend's shoulder and nearly squealed, Heather elbowed her. There were still other people in the room, and Krauss might return at any minute. Jenn got the message.

Heather learned Joe Ellis had started his professional career after graduating from Arizona State University. He spent his first five years in the majors with the Cleveland Indians. Heather guessed that's how he knew Ohio and why he claimed to be from there. The encyclopedia listed his home town as Metuchen, New Jersey. It also revealed his age would now be forty.

The teen sleuth had a sudden inspiration as she remembered the scar near Dimitrio's ear. *He probably had plastic surgery! It's no wonder he tires easily at forty! It's also obvious now why Lynda Ellis said things aren't always as they seem. I'll bet she wanted to stop him.* Heather felt terribly excited but kept her emotions in check for the time being.

Among other facts, Heather discovered that Ellis had won the prestigious Cy Young Award as the American League's best pitcher in his sixth season. Then he ran into trouble. The listing said the baseball commissioner had suspended Ellis six years ago, but it didn't say why.

Heather quickly shut the book and prepared to leave the room just as John Krauss returned. He regarded her and Jenn suspiciously when Heather thanked him for use of the archives.

"Did you find what you wanted?" he asked.

"Yes. Thank you." She nodded coolly and left.

"He's changed his tune, hasn't he?" Jenn whispered on the way to the elevator.

Heather's thoughts were on something else. "Jenn, would Geoff know anything about that suspension?" She remembered the twelve-year-old was a baseball trivia expert.

"We could find out. I think he's home."

"Let's use a phone in the press box. No one should be there now," she checked her watch.

Geoff was home, and knew about Joe Ellis and the suspension. "He was a great pitcher until he got nasty," he commented. "Let me look him up in one of my books." A few minutes later he provided more details. "Ellis was pitching one night, and the umpire kept making what Ellis considered bad calls. He got hopping mad. Then, with the bases loaded, two outs in the ninth inning, and the game tied, the umpire called a ball on a full count. That walked home the winning run. Ellis was so mad he threatened the ump."

"What did he do?" asked an excited Heather.

"He said killing the umpire wasn't such a bad idea," Geoff told her. "It didn't help that Ellis had been roughing up fans who waited near his car after a game right before that. So he got thrown out of baseball." He paused. "Why the interest in Joe Ellis?"

"I'll explain it later. Thanks so much, Geoff!"

Heather hung up and told Jenn the astonishing news. What she didn't realize was that John Krauss had listened to the entire conversation on an extension phone from his office!

15

The Concrete Tomb

W hat are you going to do?" Jenn asked.

"Tell Dave Knox. I think he'll know how to handle this."

The young sportswriter directed her friend to the seating area. Then she went into the dugout. Dave Knox was interviewing the Phillies' manager. Heather waited impatiently for them to finish. Fifteen minutes later, Danny Mastrodoni ended the discussion, and Knox moved over to his young friend on the bench. Just as she started to tell him the incredible news, however, Joe Dimitrio entered the dugout and sat too close for her to say anything!

Heather felt even more frustrated at dinner. When she, Mr. Knox, and Jenn sat at an empty table in the press club, two other reporters quickly joined them.

"Can you tell him during the game?" Jenn asked when Heather walked her to the elevator following the meal.

"I'll try my best," she vowed. "Say a prayer for me, huh?"

"You bet! Should I meet you at the press gate after the game?"

"That's the plan," Heather nodded. "See you then!"

She hoped to sit next to Dave Knox during the game, but when Heather strolled into the press box, two reporters flanked him. *Just great!* she thought grimly.

"Heather!" a familiar voice called out. It was John Krauss. "I have a message for you." He handed her a folded note.

"Thanks," she muttered. Heather found a seat and read the message. It said, "I need to talk to you. Meet me by the players' exit near the bull pen after the game. Kevin Shirley." *That's odd. Maybe he wants to talk to me when there aren't other reporters around,* she guessed. *I'll have to make it quick, though. I don't want to keep Jenn waiting.*

It was a close game, but finally Pete Manning scored the winning run for the Phillies. The crowd went wild.

Just as Heather left the press box, a siren sounded down the hall. "What's that all about?" she asked a reporter.

"Someone probably pulled a fire alarm." He shrugged indifferently. "Happens all the time. Somebody'll check it out."

As Heather left the press box, an older man in a maintenance uniform hurried off the elevator. The teenager went to the playing field and headed for the cement ramp near the bull pen. The Phillies used that exit to get to their cars. She had never left the stadium that way before and wasn't sure where Kevin Shirley wanted her to meet him. None of the other players had left yet. *I hope he won't be long,* she thought. *Jenn will wonder why I'm late meeting her.*

She followed the ramp to a busy hallway where concessionaires busily replenished their supplies for the next game. As Heather stood wondering where to go next, someone asked, "Need some help?" John Krauss stood near the door to a large room.

"Have you seen Kevin Shirley? That message you gave me said to meet him somewhere out here."

"Actually, he came by a minute ago," the young man informed her.

"Where'd he go?"

Krauss pointed inside the room. "He uses the private door. It's off-limits to everyone but the boiler-room guard and the players, though." The public relations assistant lowered his voice. "I'll make an exception since the watchman left to check on a fire alarm."

Heather followed Krauss into the giant room. It was gray and noisy and hot. She saw a staircase on the far wall that led outside, but her companion paused instead before a large, open door.

"This is the private exit," Krauss pointed out. When Heather stepped inside, she knew Kevin Shirley hadn't sent that note. *Krauss had tricked her!* He blocked her exit. "I tried to win you over," he spat, "but you wouldn't play the game. You learned the truth, all right, but it won't set you free now, Heather Reed."

Then he slammed the door in her face. Heather threw all her weight at the door and pounded it with her fists. "Let me out!" she screamed. It did no good. After a few minutes, the frightened teen looked at her surroundings and grimaced. She was in a dimly-lit hallway. On the left was a concrete wall. A small sidewalk separated it from an embankment to the right. Slimy pools of stagnant green water covered the walkway, and thick spider webs clung to the fluorescent lights above. Footsteps echoed in the chamber from somewhere around a bend in the passageway, and Heather became anxious.

Joe Dimitrio—Ellis—approached her, wearing a sinister grin. "If it isn't Heather Reed," he mocked. "You almost ruined my comeback. I couldn't let you do that now, could I?"

Heather caught her breath at his evil expression. No longer did he look like the darling of the Phillies. This was his true color.

"I belong in baseball," Ellis moved closer. "I should never have been suspended. I wasn't going to kill that umpire." He laughed spitefully. "I can't say the same for you."

He yanked Heather's arm and forced her to walk through the mucky puddles. Ellis grasped her too strongly for her to break away. The green water oozed into her leather sandals, and she felt nauseous.

"What are you going to do?" she asked.

"You're going to have an accident, and you probably won't be found for years, if then. Few people even know this place exists," he sneered.

"Where are we?"

"This is the 'concrete tomb.' It makes up part of the outfield wall. And no one ever comes in here."

Heather tried to keep him talking so she could think of a way out. "How did you find out about it?"

"Never mind!" he scolded. Ellis paused before a closed door wreathed in cobwebs. When he pulled it open with one hand, the webs expanded and contracted grotesquely. Heather tried to get away, but the pitcher's grasp tightened around her slender arm. "Good riddance, Junior Detective!"

Ellis shoved her hard and slammed the door behind her. Heather fell down several steps, but she broke her headlong tumble by grabbing a railing. On the other side of the door, the ballplayer shoved a wooden plank under the doorknob to prevent the teenager's escape.

Heather climbed to the top of the stairs slowly, feeling battered, but not broken. She pushed against the door, but it wouldn't budge. The situation seemed hopeless. Heather had been in serious jams before, but not like this. Even if she did get out of this room, she was still buried in the concrete tomb.

I'm sure Joe and John will lock the door I came in, she thought sitting on the landing. *The security guard won't know I'm in here, and I doubt he could hear me if I yelled. The walls are too thick, and the noise from the boilers would muffle it anyway.* She had no idea how far the mucky passageway stretched or where it led. *Maybe there's another door on the other end,* she considered hopefully. *If I could just get out of here!* She suddenly remembered Jenn would be waiting for her at the press gate, and that gave her fresh hope. *Jenn will ask someone to look for me! The only problem is that no one comes here*, she sighed. *Still, someone besides Joe and John must know about this place.*

When the sixteen-year-old's eyes adjusted to the darkness, she explored her prison. The stairway wasn't very steep or long. She counted twelve steps. At the bottom an enormous old scoreboard leaned against the wall. When Heather stretched out her arms, she could touch the wall on the other side. She quickly withdrew her hands, however, when they attracted cobwebs. *I wonder what other creatures are in here besides me?* she shivered, especially fearing the possibility of rats.

God, I'm going to try to force this door, she prayed on her knees. *Please strengthen my arms and back. Then show me how to escape from the concrete tomb. Also let Jenn know how to help me.*

At that very moment Jenn McLaughlin glanced at her watch for the tenth time as she leaned against the wall near the press gate. Fifty-five minutes ago she had watched the Colorado Rockies' players file through on their way to the team bus, hardly realizing Heather was late. Now her friend's delay bored Jenn.

"Hasn't your buddy come yet?" asked Bob Doro, the security director. Jenn shook her head. "Don't worry," the athletic-looking man assured her. "I'll bet she got some last-minute interviews."

"I guess," she answered sullenly.

Doro hopped into his golf cart and headed for his office on the other side of the stadium near center field.

Back in the dark chamber of the concrete tomb, Heather felt exhausted from throwing her weight against the door, trying to knock it open. She felt it give a few times, only to grow too exhausted from the effort to finish the job. After catching her breath, she tried again, determined to win her freedom. To her utter amazement, the door burst open!

Heather got out and assessed her situation. It didn't seem possible to leave by the same door she had come in, so she decided to walk in the other direction. *I'll scream a lot, too,* she determined. *It can't hurt, and someone may hear me in spite of what Joe said.* She doubted he or Krauss would be lurking about. *They probably high-tailed it out of here.*

Heather walked carefully at the base of the embankment to avoid the watery mire on the sidewalk. She didn't want to step in that water again. Mosquitoes dined on her exposed legs, and she swatted at them. As the passage stretched almost forever, the sidewalk became dry. Every few yards she screamed at the top of her lungs to alert anyone who might hear her. Heather kept this up until she became totally hoarse.

As Bob Doro sat behind his desk filling out post-game reports, he heard strange cries. *It sounds like cats,* he thought. *They're probably roaming behind the center field barrier again.*

That happened every season, and no one had captured the strays. He smiled, remembering how a black cat would show up on the field every once-in-awhile during a game. The fans and players got a big kick out of it.

As the yowling continued, however, the middle-aged man became less sure it was the cats. Then he had a sudden revelation. *That girl at the press gate said her friend hadn't shown up. I wonder. . . .* The security director hastily rode his cart back to the press gate. The girl was still there, and fear had replaced her impatience.

"Hop in!" he called out, and Jenn obeyed. "Let's look for your pal. What's her name?"

"Heather Reed. She's a sportswriter for *The Kirby Courier.*"

He nodded. "I know who you mean."

On the way to the playing field Jenn disclosed what Heather had discovered earlier about Joe Dimitrio. The security chief wore a solemn expression as he listened. He didn't tell the young woman beside him that her friend might be in real danger.

Doro parked near the visitors' bull pen and told Jenn to follow him. "She might be lost behind center field," he explained. "In my office I heard noises coming from that direction."

He went exploring behind the outfield fence where the Eagles stacked bleachers for their football games. Jenn saw many potential hiding places, but Heather wasn't in them, and there was no more screaming. When they exited at the Phillies bull pen, Doro took Jenn back to the boiler room and asked the guard if he had seen the teenager. He shook his head.

"In my office I heard a sound like cats howling," Doro raised his voice to be heard above the noise. "But I think it might've been the girl. Hey, wait a minute!" He snapped his fingers. "Chet, you know that place called the concrete tomb?" The guard nodded. "Maybe she's trapped in it!"

"That isn't likely," the man said. "Nobody goes back there."

Doro told Jenn about the "tomb." "It's 500 feet long and stretches from that door," he pointed, "to just past the visitors' bull pen. Years ago the Phillies used it for storage. Only Keith Filmore, the stadium operations manager, goes inside once in a blue moon for a quick inspection." He faced the guard. "Chet, get your key to that padlock on the door, and we'll look inside."

Chet reached for the key where others hung from a pegboard. "It's missing!" he cried.

Jenn felt panicky, but Bob Doro kept his cool. "Find Keith, and ask him to get another key to that door. I'll get one from my office, and we'll enter the tomb from the other side. Oh, and notify the police. Have them search the stadium."

They hurried out of the suffocating boiler room and took Doro's golf cart across the outfield. He parked near the visitors' bull pen. He and Jenn were about to head for his office when they heard loud banging. Doro listened closely. When he figured where the sounds were coming from, he walked quietly to a storage area next to the bull pen. Then the sound stopped.

Jenn cautiously followed. She climbed over discarded stadium seats, wooden risers, huge pieces of astroturf, and the goal posts. Suddenly more banging erupted from above them. Jenn looked up and screamed at the top of her lungs. Fifteen feet above them in the cement wall, a square opening framed Heather's grimy face. Her voice was gone, but she had attracted their attention by hitting the wall with an old bat.

"Wait there!" yelled Doro. "We'll have you out in a few minutes!"

He hurried back to his office for a special key. Then he and Jenn went to a hallway with gray metal doors held shut by a steel bar. Within minutes Heather gained her freedom. Doro took her and Jenn in his cart to the team trainer, who was just leaving.

"Please look at this girl before you go," Doro said. He quickly explained what had happened. The young trainer directed them to his office. Jenn went in with her friend. Ten minutes later the man invited Bob Doro to come in. "I think Heather will be fine after a good night's sleep," he finally pronounced.

"Which is more than I can say for Joe Dimitrio and John Krauss!" Jenn remarked.

Before leaving the Vet, Heather struggled through her hoarseness to tell a Philadelphia Police detective everything. The search for Joe (Dimitrio) Ellis and John Krauss took next to no time at all. Because they assumed Heather would die in the concrete tomb, her abductors had gone about their regular business. The police arrested the men at their homes that night.

Krauss confessed he had initiated the incident with Kevin Clausen's father and planted the drugs in Kenny

Scribner's hotel room. "Joe promised me 20 percent of his salary next year if I advanced his career," he admitted.

Joe Ellis had corked the bat Heather used during the media game, making sure it was the only one in the bin that the small teenager could handle. The pitcher also told police he deliberately injured Felix Undeljar in their practice session, but made it look like an accident. Plus, he set fire to Bib Shoon's car in the parking lot to destroy that pitcher's concentration. Because his own vehicle burned, Ellis looked innocent.

He did all those things to establish himself as the Phillies' best pitcher. That way he would have a job next season and probably a large income. The fiendish scheme ended in prison for both Ellis and Krauss.

The Phillies not only returned to normal, they won enough games to capture the National League East division title, advancing to the play-offs. Barry Webster called Heather with a special request.

"You did so much for the club's morale," he praised. "We'd like to thank you by having you throw out the first ball of the championship series when it starts next week."

"Thanks so much. I'd love to!" she exclaimed.

"Good. And you may bring five people with you," he added.

Heather invited her parents and Brian, Jenn, and Evan to the exciting game. The night of the event was crisp and moonlit. After the National Anthem the stadium announcer said, "And now Heather Reed will throw out the first ball near the Phillies' dugout."

The teenager felt nervous with all eyes fixed on her, but she threw the ball straight and hard to catcher Pete Talarri. As the Phillies fans cheered, he brought the ball back to Heather as a souvenir and kissed her on the cheek.

When Heather returned to her seat, Jenn leaned over and clapped her on the back. "I should have known a Major League mystery wouldn't be too tough for you. But what will you get into next?" she laughed.